THE BORDER VIXEN

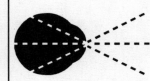

This Large Print Book carries the
Seal of Approval of N.A.V.H.

THE BORDER VIXEN

BERTRICE SMALL

THORNDIKE PRESS

A part of Gale, Cengage Learning

GALE
CENGAGE Learning·

Detroit • New York • San Francisco • New Haven, Conn • Waterville, Maine • London

LIBRARY OF CONGRESS CATALOGING-IN-PUBLICATION DATA

Small, Bertrice.
   The border vixen / by Bertrice Small.
     p. cm. — (Thorndike Press large print romance) (Border
  chronicles)
   ISBN-13: 978-1-4104-3525-5 (hardcover)
   ISBN-10: 1-4104-3525-3 (hardcover)
   1. Scotland—History—1057–1603—Fiction. 2. Large type
  books. I. Title.
  PS3569.M28B69 2011
  813'.54—dc22   2010045470

Published in 2011 by arrangement with NAL Signet, a member of
Penguin Group (USA) Inc.

For Aneta, who keeps me sane

A note for my readers: *Aisir nam Breug* is pronounced: Asher nam Breg.

PROLOGUE

Scotland, 1536

Mad Maggie Kerr could outride, outrun, outfight, outdrink, and outswear any man in the Borders. These were not, however, the virtues a gentleman looked for in a wife. But if a man liked a tall lass with dark chestnut brown hair, hazel eyes, and a fat dower, then perhaps Mad Maggie could be considered acceptable — for those reasons and the fact she was Dugald Kerr's only heir, and Dugald Kerr controlled the Aisir nam Breug.

The Aisir nam Breug was a deep, narrow passage through the border hills between Scotland and England. No one could recall a time when this transit had not been managed by the Scots Kerrs at its north end and the English Kerrs at its south end. Payment of a single toll gave the traveler the guarantee of a safe trip from one side of the border to the other. Merchants and messengers, bridal parties, and other voyagers all used the Aisir nam Breug. Warring factions did not. It had been an unspoken agreement for several centuries that the Aisir nam Breug could be used only for peaceful travel.

Management of this resource had made the Kerr family wealthy over the years. They did not, however, flaunt their wealth, but their home, set upon a low hill, was more a small castle than a tower or manor house. And the village at the foot of that hill had an air of comfortable prosperity about it that was unique in the Borders. They were loyal to the king and always ready to aid a neighbor. The Kerrs of Brae Aisir were considered both honorable and trustworthy.

But the old laird was certainly in his final days. He was the last legitimate male in his line, with a stubborn girl just turned seventeen as his only heir. And despite her reputation, which had earned her the sobriquet of Mad Maggie, Dugald Kerr needed to find his granddaughter a husband — a man who would be strong enough to hold the Aisir nam Breug for the son he would sire on Mad Maggie. It would not be an easy task, but the laird of Brae Aisir knew exactly the kind of man who could tame his lass. Finding him was another matter, however, and this man would also have to win her respect, for Maggie was proud.

"He must be able to outride, outrun, and outfight her," Dugald Kerr declared to David, his younger brother, who was the family's priest.

"I suppose yer right, Brother," David Kerr said with a small smile, "but 'twill nae be easy finding such a man. I shall have to pray mightily on this."

The laird gave a snort of laughter. "Aye," he agreed, "ye will."

"How will ye go about it, Brother?" the priest inquired.

"I'll give a feast and invite all the neighbors. Then I'll announce my intentions to them. I know Maggie frightens many of them, for she is outspoken and headstrong, but surely the lure of the Aisir nam Breug will tempt them to overlook these faults."

"She's nae as bad as she pretends," Father David said. "Yer household runs smoothly because of her. She knows how to direct the servants and care for the sick. She's nae fearful of hard work. I've seen her myself in yer fields, and working with the women salting meat for the winter, and making jams."

"She'd rather hunt the meat than prepare it," the laird said with a chuckle.

"Aye, Brother, she would," the priest

11

agreed. "But she can do what a woman with a large household needs to do. She will make the right lad a fine wife. But I don't believe you'll find that lad among the Borders, Dugald."

"I must begin my search somewhere," the laird of Brae Aisir said.

CHAPTER 1

"The hall is full, I suppose," Maggie Kerr said to her tiring woman, Grizel.

"Aye," came the tart reply. "All come to stuff themselves and get drunk at yer grandfather's board," Grizel snorted. "Armstrongs and Elliots, Bruces and Fergusons, Scotts and Bairds who are forever telling the story of how their ancestor saved the life of King William the Lion and thus gained their lands. There are a few Lindsays, and Hays too, and nae one of them fit to wipe the mud from yer boot, my darling lass."

"Maybe I'll nae join them," Maggie said. "I dislike being presented as Grandsire's prize mare." She reached for the cake of scented soap on the rim of her tall oak bathing tub and rubbed it slowly over her arm. "I don't want to marry, and I am more than capable of holding the Aisir nam Breug myself without interference from a stranger calling himself my lord and master. Jesu,

13

why wasn't I born a lad?"

"Because ye were born a lass," Grizel said matter-of-factly. "Now finish yer bath. Ye have to get down to the hall sooner than later. I'll nae let you shame your grandsire, my dearie. Nor would ye do it. Ye know yer duty better than any."

Then Grizel went and laid out the burgundy velvet gown that Maggie would wear that evening. It was high-waisted and had a low scooped neckline that revealed most of her shoulders. The tight-fitting sleeves and the hem of the gown were trimmed in dark marten. The servant set out a pair of round-toed sollerets covered in the same velvet as the gown and burgundy silk stockings with matching garters.

As Maggie stepped out of her tub, Grizel hurried to wrap her in a warmed towel. "Sit down, and let me prepare you. Then we'll put on your chemise, and you can choose the jewels you would wear. You should show to your best advantage, my dearie."

"God's balls!" Maggie swore. "Ye too, Grizel? I don't care if one of those fools asks for my hand or not. I don't want a husband, and I shall make it very difficult for any man to please me enough to win my favor." She pulled on her soft linen chemise.

Smiling to herself, Grizel gently pushed

the girl down on a stool and began to brush out her hair while Maggie dried her feet. "Yer a Kerr," she said as she plied the boar bristles through Maggie's thick chestnut-colored tresses. "Ye'll do what ye must for the good of the family."

Maggie snorted at her tiring woman's words. Grizel was like a mother to her, as her own mother had perished giving birth to her, and her father had died in a border clash six months before she was born. Grizel had lost her husband in that same fray, and her own infant son about the time Maggie entered the world. Grandsire had brought the nineteen-year-old widow up from the village to wet-nurse his new granddaughter. She had been born strong, Dugald Kerr said. There had been no doubt she would survive.

And when she no longer needed nourishment from Grizel's teat, the wet nurse had remained to raise the child for the laird of Brae Aisir. Maggie loved Grizel dearly, and she hated to disappoint her. She would go into her grandsire's hall the coming evening and be shown to prospective buyers as if a blood mare at a horse fair, but she would wed no man who could not gain her respect. And there was none among the young men she knew who had ever even been able to command her attention. They were a rough-spoken lot, and she knew their only interest in her was the Aisir nam Breug. Maggie pulled on her silk stockings, fastening the ribbon garters to hold them up.

"Let's get yer gown on," Grizel said, and she helped Maggie into the rich, soft velvet, seeing that the tight fur-cuffed sleeves fitted without a wrinkle, then lacing up the garment. The high waist of the gown forced the girl's breasts up so that they were quite visible above the low neckline. The fabric of the skirt fell in graceful folds.

"Give me my rope of pearls," Maggie said.

Grizel opened the jewel casket and drew out the pearls as her young mistress picked out several rings, which she put on her fingers. The tiring woman slid the pearls over Maggie's head. "They look just lovely," she told the lass.

"Braid my hair now in a single plait," Maggie instructed.

"I will nae do it!" Grizel said vehemently. "Yer grandsire said ye were to leave yer tresses loose this evening. I've a gold ribbon band with a small oval of polished red quartz for ye to wear as a headpiece."

"Christ Almighty! The mare is to be presented as never mounted," Maggie swore.

16

"Well, ye never have," Grizel said sharply, "though yer wild behavior has left many wondering. So ye'll do as yer told, Maggie Kerr, and nae shame yer grandsire or yer clan's good name this night."

Maggie laughed. Grizel rarely scolded her so severely. "Oh, very well. My hair shall fall about me like that of a fourteen-year-old lass, for not only am I willful, at seventeen I am fast growing out of my breeding cycle," Maggie teased the older woman. "So let my suitors think I am a helpless creature. If they would delude themselves."

Now it was Grizel who laughed. But then she secured Maggie's long hair with the gold ribbon band. "Put yer shoes on, and yer ready to make yer entrance," she said.

Maggie slipped her feet into the pretty slippers, then stood up. "You realize," she said to Grizel, "that I will frighten all those clansmen in the hall with my grand entry. I'm not the usual border woman in her one good gown trying to please. I'm the heiress to Brae Aisir, and I won't let them forget it."

"Dinna," Grizel replied. "The man who wins you will love you and respect your position. He must be worthy of you, my lass. You must nae accept a lesser man. Beware, however, of those who will try to seduce you to gain an advantage over you."

Maggie laughed. "I have managed to hold on to my virtue for seventeen years, Grizel. I will continue to hold it from those lusting after my wealth, my body, and my family's power. I can tell you that I know the man I must eventually wed is nae in Grandsire's hall this night." She reached out to take the hand of the older woman. "Come along now, Grizel. To the hall! It should prove an amusing evening."

They left the girl's rooms and descended the winding stairs. Maggie's apartment was in the southwest corner of her grandfather's home. They entered the great hall, Grizel shoving the men crowding the large room aside so her mistress might get through to the high board, where her grandfather was awaiting her arrival.

Dugald Kerr watched her come. There was pride in his brown eyes, and his mouth quirked with his amusement. The wicked wench had dressed to intimidate, and by the open mouths he could now see as he looked out over his hall, she had been successful in her attempt. She was fair enough to evoke lust in not just a few of the men there. But she did not come eyes downcast, shrinking away from his guests. She strode with the sureness of who she was — Margaret Kerr; his only heir, and closest blood relation other than his brother, David.

He was proud of her, especially because he had never expected that his frail, weak daughter-in-law, dead with Maggie's birth, could have given him any heir, let alone such a strong lass as Maggie. His youngest son, Robert, had married Glynis Kerr, one of the Netherdale Kerrs. After several centuries, they were but distantly related. Unfortunately Glynis had proved frail. She lost two sons before Maggie had been born. When Robert had been killed in the early days of Glynis's confinement, Dugald Kerr had despaired.

His two older sons, their wives, and their children were dead. The eldest of his three sons, like the youngest, had died in the border wars. He had been newly wed, and his wife had not yet borne a bairn. She had returned to her family and made another marriage. His middle son had succumbed with his wife, and two little boys, to a winter epidemic. Robert had been sixteen then. A year later he was wed, and three years later he was dead. His wife, however, understanding the gravity of the family's situation, had forced her sorrow away from her until she could birth her child safely. But seeing her father-in-law's face when the child slid from her body, Glynis had whispered but two words, "I'm sorry," loosened her hold on life, and died.

Watching Glynis's daughter now make her way to the high board, Dugald Kerr wished Glynis had lived to see the magnificent heiress she and Robbie had given Brae Aisir. He smiled broadly as Maggie stepped up and, greeting her great-uncle David first, bent and kissed Dugald Kerr's ruddy cheek. Then she settled herself into the high-backed oak chair at his right hand and gazed out over the assembly.

"Is there anyone in the Borders not eating at your expense tonight, Grandsire?" she asked mischievously, her hazel eyes dancing wickedly.

"Yer husband might be among that pack of borderers, lass," he replied, smiling at her. Maggie was, he had to admit to himself, his weakness. It was why he had allowed her to run rampant throughout the Borders. Her daring and independence delighted him, although he was wise enough to know it would not have in any other woman.

"There's nae a man in this hall tonight whom I would wed and bed, Grandsire," she told him candidly.

"It's a woman's place to marry," David Kerr said softly to her.

"Why? Because we are weak and frail vessels, Uncle? Because we are told that God created man first, and therefore we are less in his eyes? If we are less, then why is it our responsibility to bear new life to God's glory?" Maggie demanded of him.

"Why must ye always ask such damned intelligent questions, Niece?" the priest asked. His eyes, however, were dancing with amusement.

"Because I love stymieing ye, Uncle. I refuse to fit the church's mold that women are lesser creatures, fit but to keep house and spawn new souls. I do not want a husband taking precedence over me at Brae Aisir. I am perfectly capable of managing the Aisir nam Breug, and need no stranger to do it for me," Maggie said firmly.

"And when ye have left this earth, who will be left to care for the Aisir nam Breug, Maggie?" the laird asked her quietly.

She caught his hand up and kissed it. "We will be here forever, Grandsire," she said to him. "Ye and I will look after the Aisir nam Breug together."

"That is a child's reasoning," Dugald Kerr replied. "Yer no longer a child, Maggie. Ye need a husband to father a child upon ye. A child who will one day inherit what the Kerrs of Brae Aisir have kept safe for centuries. I will not force ye to the altar, but sooner or later ye must choose a man to wed. And I will help ye to find the right man, Granddaughter. One who will respect ye. One whom ye can respect."

"Nae in this hall tonight, Grandsire," she answered him.

"Perhaps ye are correct, but before we cast our nets afield, Maggie, we must give our neighbors the opportunity to woo ye," the laird said.

Maggie picked up the silver goblet studded in green malachite by her hand, and drank a healthy draft of the red wine in it. "I cannot gainsay ye, Grandsire," she told him. "Very well; let us see what we may find from this showing of lads all eager to win my hand, spend my fortune, and take my inheritance." And she laughed.

"God help the man who finally pleases ye," David Kerr said dryly.

The laird laughed and signaled his servants to begin bringing the meal. They streamed into the hall, bearing steaming platters, dishes, and bowls of food. The trestle tables below the high board where the three Kerrs sat had been set with linen cloths, polished pewter plates, and tankards filled with good strong ale. There were round loaves of bread upon the tables, small wheels of hard cheese, and crocks of sweet butter. The servants offered poultry, fish, boar, and venison, which the male guests greedily ate up. Few of the vegetables offered were consumed by the clansmen, who were content with well-cooked meat, fish, game, bread, and cheese.

At the high board the dishes were more varied, and while it was meat, game, and seafood, it was more delicately offered. Trout braised in white wine and set upon green watercress was offered along with a bowl of steamed prawns. There was a roasted duck stuffed with dried apples and bread, and roasts of lamb, boar, and venison. Bowls of peas and a salad of lettuces were presented. The high board had a large round cottage loaf, butter, and two cheeses — one from France that was soft and creamy, the other a good hard yellow cheese.

Maggie watched as the guests wolfed down everything offered to them and quaffed tankard after tankard of brown ale. Some of the men had more delicate manners than others. The clansmen barely mingled, sitting at their own tables and eyeing one another suspiciously. She wondered how long it would be before a fight would break out, but she knew her grandsire's men-at-arms now lining the hall could handle any unpleasant situation. The high board was cleared, and a sweet was brought for Maggie. Cook had made for her a custard with jam, which Maggie very much favored.

Her grandfather waited for her to finish the treat before he stood up. Instantly the hall quieted. " 'Tis good to have ye all here with us tonight," Dugald Kerr said, and he smiled down at them. He was a handsome man in his sixties not yet bowed by his years. He was clean shaven and had a full head of white hair cut short, a long face and nose, and sharp brown eyes. He wore a long dark tunic brocaded in gold and trimmed with marten. No one would have ever mistaken the laird of Brae Aisir for anything other than what he was — a wealthy man.

"As you must surely know, I am growing older," he began. "My only heir is my granddaughter, Margaret. I hope to find a husband for her among ye. However, I will not give her to another lightly. To win her hand ye must be able to outride, outrun, and outfight Maggie. Ye must win her respect. Now, should any of ye wish to put yerselves forth as a possible husband for my granddaughter, come and speak with me before ye depart on the morrow. The man who weds and beds my Maggie will one day control the Aisir nam Breug. But if I can find none among ye who suits her or me, know that I will look elsewhere, but the same conditions will apply. Now drink up, and let my piper entertain you all." Dugald Kerr sat back down.

A murmuring arose in the hall now, and Maggie almost laughed as speculative glances were cast in her direction by the men below. As it had been guessed that the laird of Brae Aisir was seeking a husband for his granddaughter, many of the other clan lords had come with the sons they had of marriageable age. And several of the lairds themselves were unmarried, or widowers seeking a second or third wife.

" 'Tis a goodly selection," her priestly great-uncle murmured. "Lord Hay's brother looks a possible match for you."

"I prefer a younger man whom I may control," Maggie said low. "One who will be content to let me do what needs doing while taking all the credit. I care naught for recognition. I just want the Aisir nam Breug managed properly. If I spawn a son I can teach, then I will do so. But none out there looks to possess any wits at all."

"Ye cannot judge by just looking at them," her grandfather remarked. "Let the piper play, and dance with a few of them. Perhaps you will be surprised."

"More likely I will be disappointed, but I will take your advice, Grandsire," Maggie replied. Then rising, she called out, "Who will dance with me, my lords?" And she stepped from the dais to be suddenly surrounded by a group of eager males. Looking them all over with a bold eye she smiled, then addressed a young man with pale blond hair. "Ye will do to start with," she said, holding out a graceful hand.

He eagerly grasped the hand and said almost breathlessly, "Calum Lindsay, Mistress Maggie." His other arm slipped about her waist as the piper began to play a lively tune. He was unfortunately not a good dancer, tripping first over his own feet, and then hers. He looked to be no more than sixteen, and his Adam's apple bobbed nervously up and down in his throat as he concentrated on the quick steps of the country dance. Not once did he dare to meet her glance, for he found he was intimidated by the beautiful girl.

Maggie's chestnut brown hair was tossed about as they danced. It was impossible to engage Calum Lindsay in conversation, as she could see if he had to speak with her, he would lose his concentration with the dance. She was relieved when an older man stepped in to partner her, cutting the lad out to the boy's obvious relief. Maggie looked directly at the gentleman, recognizing the red plaid of Clan Hay. "And ye are?" she asked.

"Ewan Hay," he replied shortly as they capered across the hall with quick steps and turned sharply. He lifted her up, swinging her about before returning Maggie's feet to the floor. "I am twenty-eight, have never been wed, am a third son, and will speak with your grandsire on the morrow."

"Indeed," Maggie replied. "And think ye that ye can outride, outrun, and outfight me, Ewan Hay?"

"Yer a woman, for Christ's sake," he responded. "Oh, I've heard of yer reputation, but 'tis certainly bragging, madam, and nothing more."

Maggie laughed. "God's balls, sir, what a fool ye be if ye believe that! Still, ye are welcome to speak with my grandsire. Nothing will give me greater pleasure than to beat ye in all three contests."

Ewan Hay's face darkened with anger. "We will see, madam, just how ye fare in a contest with me. And when I have put ye in yer proper place, and wed ye, I shall on our wedding night take a sturdy hazel switch and whip the pride out of ye. Ye will learn how to behave like a proper wife in my charge."

"I would nae wed ye if ye were the last man on the face of the earth," Maggie said angrily. "Remember my words when I blood ye with my blade." When the music stopped she pulled away from him and returned to the high board.

"Yer flushed," Dugald Kerr noted. "Did Lord Hay's younger brother say something to distress ye?"

"He will sue for my hand, beat me in all three contests, and whip me with a hazel on our wedding night so I learn my proper place," Maggie told her grandsire and her great-uncle.

The laird's head snapped up. He looked about until he could find Ewan Hay, then glared at him. "I shall nae accept his suit," he said angrily.

"Nay, let him try to best me," Maggie said in a cold, even voice. "He is a man who wants public humiliation, and I shall enjoy giving it to him. Let the bastard try to beat me in fair combat. I shall enjoy shaming him before the rest of them."

"Be careful, Niece," David Kerr said warily.

"I will, Uncle," Maggie replied. She rose

again. "Now, sirs, if ye will excuse me, I have had enough tonight and would beg yer leave to depart the hall."

"Ye have it," her grandfather said. "Rest well, my bairn."

Maggie departed the great hall, moving quickly through and past the tables below the board. She had eaten sparingly and drunk little. Tomorrow, when Ewan Hay sought to gain her hand in marriage, she intended pressing him into the battle immediately. Under the best of conditions she could beat him, but he had poured a lot of ale into himself tonight, and she didn't doubt for one moment that after their meeting he had been tempted to swill more like the pig he was. She smiled wickedly to herself. She must get to bed immediately. A good night's rest was necessary to teaching Lord Hay's younger brother the lesson he needed to learn.

Grizel was waiting for her, and she listened as Maggie shared the details of the evening with her. "That Hay laddie is too bold for my taste," she said.

"He won't be quite so bold by this time tomorrow," Maggie said grimly.

"Be careful, my lass. A fellow like that is not to be trifled with, I fear," Grizel said.

"They are said to be hard men, the Border Hays."

"Wake me at first light," Maggie said as she finished undressing. She washed her face, hands, and teeth before climbing into her comfortable bed hung with rose-colored velvet curtains.

"I will," Grizel promised as she put her mistress's clothing away. Then she hurried from the bedchamber while behind her Maggie blew out the taper by her bed.

As morning began to lighten the sky some hours later, Grizel returned to awaken the girl. Maggie jumped from her bed at once, rested and ready for her challenge. Instructing her serving woman, she pulled on a pair of dark-colored breeks, tucking her chemise into the pants and donning a white linen shirt that she carefully laced up. Then she sat pulling on a pair of light woolen stockings, and her worn leather boots. "I'll go to the kitchens and get some hot oats," she said to Grizel, and ran off.

The cook filled a bowl with oat stir-about. Maggie shaved some sugar from the sugar cone the cook offered over her oats and poured heavy cream atop it. Then taking up her spoon, she quickly ate the porridge.

"A slice of fresh cottage loaf, mistress?" the cook asked.

"Just the oats. I think I will be running this morning," Maggie said.

The cook cackled. "The server says Lord Hay's brother is engaging the laird in conversation right now. I saw him last night. He has a handsome face, but he used one of the serving lasses hard. His heart is a cruel one."

"Dinna fear," Maggie answered the woman. "I'll nae have him." Then finished with her oats, she hurried up the stairs to the great hall where Lord Hay and his brother, Ewan, were speaking with the laird. Maggie bounded right up to her grandfather's side, where she stood looking boldly down at the two men.

"Ewan Hay would have yer hand, lass," Dugald Kerr said.

"Is he willing to meet our terms, Grandsire?" Maggie asked quietly.

"He says he is," came the reply.

"Today?" Maggie said pointedly. "I dinna like him, Grandsire, and I would quickly put his hopes to an end."

"Today? Are ye mad?" Ewan Hay burst out. "Ye indulge the wench, my lord, far too much. When we are wed I will nae indulge her so."

"If ye wish to try to win me, sir, it will be on my grandsire's terms, and nae yers,"

Maggie said coldly. "Today, tomorrow, next week. Ye will nae overcome me, and frankly I should just as soon be quit of ye today as tomorrow."

"My lord?" Ewan Hay turned to the laird.

"She's correct, young Hay. So if ye want her, ye will take up the challenge this day. If ye canna win her today, ye will nae be able to win her another day — believe me."

Ewan Hay turned to his elder brother, but Lord Hay shook his head, saying, "The laird knows whereof he speaks. If ye really want her, then best her this day and be done with it, Ewan. If ye choose nae to, ye canna be blamed if ye dinna want to face this challenge. There are other lasses more biddable for ye to wed than this one."

"I will nae be beaten by a woman," Ewan Hay snarled, his face darkening when Maggie laughed aloud.

"We will run barefoot," she said sweetly.

"Barefoot?" His voice went up a full octave.

" 'Tis my way, sir." Then she sat down at the high board, swiftly removing her boots and stockings.

"Decline the challenge, and let us go home," Lord Hay said to his brother.

"Never!" Ewan Hay almost shouted.

The course they would race both on foot and by horse was to be the same. They would go across the drawbridge, down the hill, run straight through the village, turn about, and come back up the hill again to circle the little keep once before crossing the drawbridge once more. As soon as they returned, they would mount up and redo the identical route a-horse. There would be no stopping.

"And if ye survive the races," Maggie said, "I will engage ye in swordplay. The match is over when one of us draws blood. Do ye agree?"

"Aye!" Ewan Hay said through gritted teeth. When he had met her challenge and won, he would beat her black and blue on their wedding night for her boldness this day. He yanked off his shoes and stockings.

"Ye hae small feet," Maggie noted. "They say a man with small feet has a small cock, sir."

Lord Hay swallowed back his laughter as his younger sibling's face darkened again with outrage. The lass was baiting him nicely into anger. If he succumbed to that anger, he would drain his energy, but then that was precisely what the girl intended.

He did not expect he would be welcoming Mad Maggie Kerr into their family.

The hall emptied out into the yard and to the drawbridge. Grizel hurried up to her mistress to tie her hair back with a red ribbon. Then Dugald Kerr asked both combatants if they were ready. Gaining their acquiescence, he raised his hand up and dropped the white napkin he had been holding. It fluttered to the ground as Ewan Hay and Maggie Kerr sprinted off to the cheers of the onlookers.

But it was obvious from the beginning that the man could not outrun the girl.

She was almost out of sight before he reached the end of the drawbridge. He winced with each pebble that his foot struck, swearing softly as he tried to run to catch up with her. At the end of the village were two Hay clansmen waiting to verify that both parties had gone the full length. Maggie passed him going in the other direction.

"Bitch!" he shouted at her as she dashed by, and he heard her laughter.

Maggie gave it her all. She wanted this over and done with. Regaining the courtyard, she did not even pause to put her boots back on, although she had more than enough time to do so. She leaped upon the back of her dapple gray stallion and raced from the courtyard, leaning low upon the beast, her bare heels digging into the animal's side. She passed Ewan Hay as he stumbled up the hill to encircle the castle. It was over, and she knew it, but she knew he would not admit defeat until she blooded him with her blade. She was actually looking forward to it, but she was denied the pleasure, for when she rode back into the courtyard, Ewan Hay was seated upon a step, Grizel tending to his bleeding feet. He had not even bothered to mount his horse.

Maggie slid from her horse and walked over to him. "Do ye admit defeat, sir?" she asked him coldly. "Ye completed but one of the three challenges."

"Madam, despite yer wealth, and the power ye will hold, I would nae hae ye for a wife if ye were the last woman on the face of God's green earth," Ewan Hay said grimly. "Yer a border vixen, and I pity the man, if he even exists, who will tame, wed, and bed ye. Is that a stallion ye were riding just now?" He stared, surprised.

"Aye," Maggie drawled, smiling. She bent to pull her stockings and boots back on.

Ewan Hay shook his blond head. "A woman who rides a stallion is nae the lass for me," he admitted to her, briefly humbled.

"Ye ran a good race," Maggie said generously.

He looked up at her and shook his head.

Then he said to Grizel, "Can ye help me get my boots on, woman?"

"Yer feet are too swollen, sir," Grizel said. "I'll wrap them for ye, but ye'll nae wear yer boots for the next few days."

Ewan Hay swore beneath his breath. "How am I to ride?" he asked of no one in particular. He stared at his neatly bound feet.

"We'll get ye on yer mount," Dugald Kerr said. He did not invite either Lord Hay or his brother back into the keep. "See to it," the laird told the captain of his men-at-arms. Then he turned to his granddaughter. "The men yer training are waiting, lass."

"Aye, Grandsire," Maggie said, going off to drill a small squad of lads awaiting her in the courtyard. She tossed the reins of her stallion to one of the stable boys as she went.

Dugald Kerr gave a final glance to the Hays. "I thank ye for coming," he said. Then he turned away and returned to his hall where throughout the morning he bid his guests farewell. Most of them had watched as Ewan Hay had been humiliated and soundly beaten. None of them stepped forward to speak with the laird other than to thank him for his hospitality. When the last of them had departed, Dugald Kerr sighed, saying to his priestly brother, "I know Maggie is a formidable lass, David, but are all of our border lads such weaklings that they would not even attempt to meet the challenges set forth?"

"Nae after seeing the Hay beaten so thoroughly," David Kerr said. "Why must ye insist on a husband for Maggie meeting such a challenge?"

"She will nae love or respect a man who cannot best her. Her husband will need her help, her guidance, in managing the Aisir nam Breug. There isn't a man in my house, in my ranks, on my lands, who does not respect Mad Maggie Kerr. There are some who even fear her, David. And they are right too. What a pity she was not born a lad!"

"She's more lad than lassie," the priest said dryly, "but I suppose yer right. She'll need a strong man by her side. But after today's exhibition, I dinna know who'll have her. I will pray on it, however, Dugald."

In the weeks that followed, several of the border lords sent to the laird of Brae Aisir; some even returned to speak with him face-to-face in an effort to negotiate a marriage contract between one of their kinsmen and Mad Maggie Kerr. But Dugald Kerr remained firm in his resolve. The man who married his granddaughter had to vanquish her, and earn her respect. Turned away, the lairds finally met at a small inn in the border hills to discuss the matter of Dugald Kerr, Mad Maggie, and the Aisir nam Breug.

"If the old man dies," one laird said, "what will happen to the traverse? It can't be left in the hands of a flighty lass."

"We all know the girl must be wed," another laird said, "but who is brave enough to force the lass?"

"David Kerr knows enough to hold the Aisir nam Breug," a voice spoke up.

"He's a priest. Do we want the church controlling the passage?" another said.

"Dugald Kerr looked sound of both body and mind to me," a man remarked.

"Aye!" several voices agreed.

"Perhaps we hae best leave things as they are right now," an Elliot clansman said.

"The lass is ripe for marriage, and if some of the younger lads were to court her, mayhap she would forget her foolishness and choose one of them."

There were murmurs of assent from the majority of the men in the small inn. They drank a toast to their decision, then scattered in different directions. But Ewan Hay sat brooding over his tankard. He had considered kidnapping the vixen while she was out riding, forcing her to his will, and impregnating her. She would have to wed him then or suffer the shame of bearing a bastard. She would be ruined for any other man and have no choice but to accept him. But such an action was apt to cause a feud between the Hays and the Kerrs. His elder brother had warned him against such an action. He would more than likely end up being killed himself, he said to Lord Hay in an attempt to reassure him that he would not act in a precipitous manner.

"I'll kill ye myself, Ewan, if ye shame the Kerr lass," Lord Hay warned. "Find another way if ye really want her. I'm not averse to the Hays controlling the Aisir nam Breug. It's made the Kerrs wealthy. I should enjoy a bit of that wealth."

"I could go to the king," Ewan Hay said to his brother. "I could tell him how old Kerr is coming to his end. Of how a man is needed to watch over such a valuable resource, and the laird has but a frail granddaughter for an heir."

Lord Hay considered his younger brother's reasoning. "Aye," he said slowly. " 'Tis just possible ye might gain an advantage if ye went to the king. The rest of them are trying to figure out how to get around old Dugald Kerr. This might be the way, and the first man to the post is likely to gain the prize. Aye! Go to the king, Ewan."

So Ewan Hay took his horse, and a dozen men-at-arms, and rode to Linlithgow where the king, James V, was now in residence.

James Stewart was twenty-four. He was a tall big-boned man with short hair, and icy cold eyes. His features were sharply drawn and fine with a narrow long nose much like an eagle's beak. Still, he was considered an attractive fellow by the women of the court and already had several mistresses, for he had charm. His charm, however, did not run deep. He was known to be ruthless when he wanted his way. James V was not a man who excited loyalty. The earls and the lairds did not like the king, for he was a hard and greedy man. His common folk loved him. At the moment, the king was contemplating taking a queen, considering candidates from Italy, France, and even Denmark, from where his paternal grandmother had come.

Lord Hay had warned his brother to tread lightly, but Ewan Hay was eager to take his revenge upon Mad Maggie Kerr. He could think of nothing but her fury and frustration when the king ordered her to marry him. And so, having managed to gain a few moments of the king's time, Ewan Hay went to court, dressed in his finest tunic.

"Who is he?" the king asked his page as

Ewan approached him confidently.

"The brother of Lord Hay, a border lord. He's unimportant, my liege."

"Then why am I speaking with him?" the king wanted to know.

"He said the matter is of great importance to Scotland," the page murmured.

Ewan Hay had reached the chair where the king sat. He smiled toothily and then bowed low. "My liege, I appreciate your seeing me," he began. His eye, however, shifted briefly to the beautiful woman who leaned against the king's chair. She had fine big breasts and full, lush lips. He forced his gaze away from her.

"What is so important to Scotland that you would ride from the border to Linlithgow to speak with me, Ewan Hay?" the king asked. He had seen the man's gaze shift to his mistress, Janet Munro.

"The future of the Aisir nam Breug is in terrible danger, my liege," Ewan began.

"What is the Aisir nam Breug, and why should I care if it is in danger?" James Stewart wanted to know.

"Why, my lord, it is a passage between Scotland and England that has for centuries been used as a safe traverse between England and Scotland. It is controlled on our side of the border by the Kerrs of Brae Aisir

41

and on the other side by their English cousins, the Kerrs of Netherdale. These two families have kept it free of warring parties so commerce and honest folk may travel between the two countries in safety. The Kerrs have become rich over the years from this passage," Ewan said.

"Indeed?" the king replied, now interested. How was it he had not known of this?

But then his border lords were very difficult and independent men. He had only just gotten firm control of them in the past few years. But, curious now, he said, "What is the problem, then, Ewan Hay?"

"The laird of Brae Aisir is in his dotage, my liege. His only heir is his granddaughter, Margaret. The lass is of marriageable age, but the old man will nae part with her. If Dugald Kerr dies, what will happen to the Aisir nam Breug with no strong man to oversee it? The girl can be given a dower for a husband, but she canna control such a valuable asset to Scotland, my liege. And what if she takes an English husband? They are a close family, Brae Aisir and Netherdale," Ewan lied, for he didn't really know.

"Are they?" the king said. What was it about this young man? From the moment he had opened his mouth, James Stewart hadn't liked him. "Would ye wed the lass?"

he asked, curious as to the answer he would receive.

"Nay, my liege. She refused my suit, and I would nae hae a wife who did not want me," Ewan said. But he would have her, he thought, if only to crush her spirit.

"But ye want her inheritance," the king remarked.

"Aye . . . nay, my liege! 'Tis my brother and all the local lairds who fear for the fate of the Aisir nam Breug. They sent me to bring this situation to your attention." He lied again, hoping it was not obvious.

"And now ye have," the king said with a small smile. "Go home, Ewan Hay. I must think on the information ye have brought to me, but rest assured that I will see the status of the Aisir nam Breug solved so that the laird of Brae Aisir may go to his God knowing that both it and his granddaughter are in safe hands."

Ewan opened his mouth to speak further, but the king waved a dismissive hand at him, and the king's page was immediately at Ewan's elbow escorting him from the royal presence before he might say another word. It had not gone at all as he had intended, but the king had not refused his subtle request. He would go home and tell his brother that the Aisir nam Breug was near to being in their hands.

James Stewart watched him go. "A dishonest fellow, I have not a doubt," he said.

Janet Munro slid into his lap. "I didn't like him, Jamie," she said. "There is more to it than he is admitting or telling." She nuzzled his ear.

He slid a casual hand into her bodice, cupping one of her gloriously large breasts. "What would ye do, Jan?" he asked her as he caressed the soft flesh absently.

"Ye need to send someone ye can trust into the border to learn more about it before ye decide. Ye canna take that man's word for anything, I am thinking," she said.

He nodded. "Aye, but whom shall I send?"

Janet Munro thought for a long moment. Then she said, "What about yer cousin, Lord Fingal Stewart?"

"Do I know him?" the king asked. He didn't think he knew a Fingal Stewart.

"Nay, ye do not. Like ye, he descends from King Robert the Third through his elder son, David, whose bairn was born after that prince was killed and was protected by his mother's Drummond kin. He was one of the first who swore loyalty to James the First when he returned from his exile. James the First gave his nephew a house in Edinburgh. The family are called

44

the Stewarts of Torra because their house is near the castle beneath the castle rock. They have always been loyal without question, to James the Second and Third, and then to yer father, James the Fourth."

"How do ye know all of this?" the king asked his mistress.

She laughed. "Fingal's grandmam was a Munro. We're cousins. He's a good man, my lord. Honest and loyal to the bone. Tell him what ye want of him, and he will do it without question." She gave him a quick kiss on his lips.

The king withdrew his hand from Janet Munro's bodice and gently tipped her from his lap. "Send to yer cousin," he said. "I am interested to meet this relation I never knew I had. If this Aisir nam Breug is all Ewan Hay claims it is, we cannot have it fall into the wrong hands." *And it will provide me with a new source of income,* he thought to himself. A king could never have too much coin in his treasury.

Janet Munro curtsied, her claret red velvet skirts spreading out around her as she did. "Aye, my lord, I will do yer bidding," she said. And then she left him.

CHAPTER 2

In the company of six of the king's men-at-arms Janet rode to Edinburgh, going to the stone house with the slate roof that sat off the street known as the Royal Mile, below the walls of Edinburgh Castle. She had sent a messenger ahead, and Fingal Stewart was waiting for her. His serving man ushered her into a small book-filled chamber.

"I bring you greetings from yer cousin, the king," Janet said, kissing his cheek.

"I wasn't aware my *cousin,* the king, was even mindful of my existence," Fingal Stewart said wryly. "And what, pray, my pretty, does he want of me? Sit down, Jan."

"Today a border clansman came to him with an interesting tale," Janet Munro began, seating herself as she spread her skirts about her. Then she went on to tell Fingal Stewart of Ewan Hay's visit. When she had finished she said, "Neither Jamie nor I liked the fellow. He isn't telling the whole story. It's obvious the fool hopes the king will gift him with this old laird's holding because this pass is said to be valuable."

"And the heiress," Fingal Stewart murmured. Land and a woman, he considered, were always the makings of a volatile situation. There would be wealth to be gained by whoever got the lass.

"Nay! He said he didn't want the girl. He claimed she had refused his suit," Janet Munro replied. "I think he lies. He wants the lass."

"But his true interest lies in this Aisir nam Breug," Fingal Stewart said slowly. "He would get the king to disinherit the lass who turned him away for his own benefit. A prince of a fellow indeed. But what has this to do with me?"

Janet shook her head. "I'm not sure, Fingal, but I believe the king would have you go into the border to reconnoiter the situation and bring him back the truth of the matter."

"Why me?" Fingal Stewart was curious. Although he was Lord Stewart of Torra, he was but distantly related to the king. They had shared a thrice-great-grandfather, and the royal Stewarts had rewarded their small loyalty when James I came to the throne with their name, a title, and this undistinguished house. They were not wealthy, nor influential, and had no place among the court or the powerful. Fingal Stewart hired his sword out when he needed funds. His father had done the same.

The rest of the time he lived quietly, gambling with a few friends now and again and enjoying the favors of one of the town's pretty whores for a night or two. His funds did not extend much beyond that. He had been decently educated, but he had no pretensions, for there were plenty of others bearing the name Stewart who kept him from thinking he was someone special. He wasn't, and he didn't want to be.

"The king wants someone not associated with him, but he also wants someone he can trust, Fingal," Janet Munro told her cousin. "Ye are nae just his kin. Yer mine too."

He thought a moment, and then grinned. "Aye, I am related to ye both. Maire Drummond gave David Stewart, Duke of Rothsay, heir to King Robert the Third, a son. She was enceinte with the bairn when Rothsay was murdered by Albany, so James the First followed his father after his exile in England."

"The Drummonds protected the bairn whose mam died birthing him," Janet said.

"And Albany was so busy with his plotting to supplant his nephew, he forgot all about the child who grew up, married an heiress, and sired two sons and two daughters before dying in his bed at the age of fifty-four," Fingal said.

"Which of the sons do you descend from?" Janet asked, curious.

"The elder, who was christened Robert after his father. He had a son, David, who wed Jane Munro, and sired James, who sired me at the advanced age of fifty-six."

"God's mercy," Janet exclaimed. "I did not know that! How old was yer mam?"

"Sixteen," Fingal Stewart said. "She was the granddaughter of an old friend. Her entire family was wiped out in a winter plague. She had nothing, so she sent to my father, begging his help. There was nothing for it but to marry her, for she had virtually naught to bring any man for a dower. Even the church did not want her. I was conceived on their wedding night. My father wanted to be sure that my mother was safe if he died because, while he was hardly a wealthy man, he did have this house and a small store of coin with the goldsmith. He believed if they shared a child, none would dispute her rights. And she loved him, strange to say. She died when I was ten."

"But your father lived to be eighty," Janet

Munro said. "I remember my father remarking upon it. He said he had never known a man to live that long."

"Do ye love him?" Lord Stewart asked her, suddenly changing the subject entirely. "Do you love James Stewart, Jan?"

Janet Munro thought a moment, and then she said, "James Stewart is nae a man who inspires love, but I like him well enough, and he is good to me. He wants a lover who pleases him and asks little of him. Actually he is more generous that way." She laughed. "My influence with him is coming to an end, for he plans to go to France in the autumn. He wants a queen, and Marie de Bourbon, daughter of the Duke of Vendôme, is available. I have just discovered I am enceinte, and so I will retire to my father's house when the king leaves, and only return at his invitation, which is unlikely. He will nae offend his new queen, nor would I make an enemy of her."

Fingal Stewart nodded. "When would he see me?" he asked.

"Come back to Linlithgow with me today," she said.

He nodded. "Very well," he agreed. "I suppose today is as good a day as any. But first I must see if Archie can find me more respectable garb in which to meet the king."

"I'm not sure ye have a good enough garment to go to the court," Archie said dourly when asked. Turning to Janet Munro, the serving man complained, "I keep telling him he must keep one fine thing, but he says the expense is not worth it." He sighed. "I'll see what I can find for him, my lady."

"He's quite devoted to you," Janet noted with a small smile.

"He fusses like an old woman with one chick," Fingal replied.

Archie managed to dress his master in a pair of brown and black velvet canions, which were tight knee breeches. The stockings beneath them were brown, and his leather boots almost covered them. The matching black velvet doublet was embroidered with just the lightest touch of gold breaking the severity of the garment.

Standing before his cousin, Lord Stewart, now fully dressed, said, "I have no idea where he managed to obtain such garb, or keep it so well hidden from me."

Archie grinned and handed his master a dark brown woolen cloak and a pair of brown leather gloves. "I dinna steal it," he said. "Ye paid for it, my lord."

"I'm sure I did," Fingal replied.

"I had forgotten what a handsome devil ye are," Janet said. She pushed a lock of her

51

cousin's dark hair from his forehead. "Do ye have a hat for him, Archie?"

"No bloody hat," Lord Stewart said firmly, "and especially if it has one of those damned drooping feathers hanging from it."

"I saved no coin for a hat, as I know how ye feel about them," Archie said.

Together the two cousins rode the distance between the city and the king's favored palace, the men-at-arms surrounding them. The summer day was long, but it was close to sunset when they arrived. Janet Munro sent a page for the king and brought her cousin to her lover's privy chamber to await James Stewart. It was close to an hour before he came. Outside the windows of the small room the skies grew scarlet with the sunset, and then darkened. A serving man came and lit the fire in the hearth, for the evening was cool and damp with a hint of a later rain.

Finally James Stewart entered the chamber. He was a tall young man with the red-gold hair of his Tudor mother, and eyes that were gray in color but showed no expression at all. He held out his hand to Fingal Stewart, and a quick glance at Janet Munro told her she was dismissed. She curtsied and departed. "So," the king said, "I am to understand we are cousins."

"Like you, my lord, I trace my descent from Robert the Third through his elder son, David," Fingal Stewart explained. "You descend from his younger son, King James the First."

"I was not aware David Stewart had any offspring," the young king replied.

"Few were, my lord. His mistress was a Drummond. When Albany murdered him, her family protected her and the son she shortly bore. Albany was too busy consolidating his position, and frankly, I believe he forgot all about her. When King James the First returned home as a man, his cousin came and pledged his loyalty."

"A loyalty my great-great-grandfather certainly needed," the young king remarked.

"My ancestor was well schooled in loyalty to his king, and that king saw that he was legally able to take the surname of Stewart. He also gave his cousin a house in Edinburgh near the castle," Fingal told his royal companion.

"Where do the Munros come into your family tree?" the king asked.

"My grandfather married a Munro who was the sister to Janet's grandfather. I believe Jan was named for her, my lord."

The king nodded. "We are but distantly related now, you and I, Fingal Stewart, but blood is blood. Jan tells me you are loyal to me. Is that so? I am not so well loved by my earls, though the common folk revere me." He looked closely at his companion.

"I am loyal, my lord," Fingal Stewart said without a moment's hesitation.

"When my father pushed his father from the throne," the king wanted to know, "which side did Lord Stewart of Torra take then?"

"Neither side, my lord. He remained in his house below Edinburgh Castle until all was settled. He had been loyal to King James the Third and was equally loyal to King James the Fourth," Lord Stewart explained.

"A prudent man," the fifth James noted with a small chuckle. He had liked the candid answer he had received. "And ye, Fingal Stewart, are ye a prudent man?"

"I believe such can be said of me, my lord," came the quiet answer.

The king looked Lord Stewart of Torra over silently. He was a big man, taller than most, with dark hair like the Munros, clear gray eyes like his own that engaged the king's gaze without being forward, but a face like a Stewart with its aquiline nose. The king would have easily recognized this man in a crowd as one of his own family.

He trusted his mistress's advice in this matter. Janet Munro was the most sensible woman he had ever known. And he had known many women despite his youth. His stepfather, the Earl of Angus, had seen to that in an attempt to debauch him. Angus was now in exile, and his flighty Tudor mother wed to Lord Methven. However, this man now seated with James in his privy chamber was not just his kin, but kin to his reasonable and judicious mistress as well. He was not allied with any of the king's enemies. If Fingal Stewart could not be trusted, then who could be? "Jan has told you of my visitor earlier today?"

Lord Stewart nodded. "She has, my lord. She said she believed you wanted me to go into the Borders to see to the truth of the matter if it could be done discreetly."

"Aye, I had thought that was what I desired, but while Jan was gone to fetch you, *Cousin,* I thought more on it. I am not well beloved by certain families in the Borders — families allied with Angus and his traitorous Douglas kin. My justice towards them has been well deserved, but harsh, I know. If I send you into the Borders to reconnoiter the situation, someone is certain to guess why you are there.

"The situation into which I am sending

you is fraught with danger if I do not strike quickly and decisively. So I have decided you will travel with a dozen of my own men-at-arms at your back who will remain with you. You will present yourself to Dugald Kerr, the laird of Brae Aisir, and tell him I have learned of his difficulties. Then you will hand him this." He held out a tightly rolled parchment affixed with the royal seal. "I have written to the laird that I have sent him my cousin, Lord Stewart of Torra, to wed with his granddaughter, Margaret, and thus keep the Aisir nam Breug safe for future generations of travelers. The marriage is to be celebrated immediately. I dinna nae trust the laird's neighbors, especially the Hays. If the lass is wed, the matter is settled, and peace will reign. I want it settled before I leave for France in a few weeks' time."

Fingal Stewart was astounded by the king's speech. He had expected to travel cautiously into the Borders and carefully ferret out the truth of whatever situation the king needed to know about. But to be told he was to go and wed the heiress to Brae Aisir? He was briefly rendered speechless.

"Ye aren't already wed, are ye?" the king asked him. "I did not think to ask Jan." God's foot, if Lord Stewart were wed, what other could he choose? Whom could he trust?

"Nay, my lord," Fingal managed to say.

"Nor contracted?"

Lord Stewart shook his head in the negative. He was trying hard to adjust to being told to marry. How old was she? Was she pretty? Would she like him? It didn't matter. It would be done by royal command. No one disobeyed a royal command and lived to brag on it. He dared say naught until he heard more of this, and why.

"Do ye have a mistress ye will need to placate?" James Stewart wanted to know.

"I canna afford a mistress," Fingal Stewart answered the king. "I am nae a rich man, my lord. My parents are both dead. Nor do I have siblings. I have my house, but naught else. I hire out my sword to earn my living, and possess but one servant."

"So ye are free to leave Edinburgh quickly," the king said almost to himself. It was perfect. It did not occur to him that Lord Stewart might turn him down. He couldn't. This was a royal command, and to be obeyed without question.

"Aye, my lord," Fingal Stewart replied. He was agreeing to this madness because he had no other choice. It was his family's tradition to be loyal without question to their kings. Still, he made a small attempt to reason with James Stewart and learn more of what was expected of him. "Why must this lass be wed quickly, my lord? May I know what more is involved in this situation? What will the laird of Brae Aisir think of your sending a cousin to wed his heiress? What if he says nay?"

James Stewart barked a short laugh as he realized in his eagerness to solve this problem he had told Fingal Stewart little or nothing of it. "The Kerrs of Brae Aisir possess control of a pass through the Cheviots into England. The pass is called the Aisir nam Breug. Their English kin, the Kerrs of Netherdale, control the other end. The pass has always been used for peaceful travel; never for war nor raiding. The Kerrs on both sides of the border have defended it against such use. The laird is old. He has one heir, his granddaughter. She will not choose a husband from among their neighbors. Indeed, she is said to be called Mad Maggie, for she is willful and wild.

"The laird fears his neighbors will attempt to wrest his control of this crossing from him, or from his granddaughter when he is gone, but the lass has him at an impasse. He'll nae refuse my command that she take ye for a husband. If old Kerr had his own choice for the lass, the matter would have been long settled. He obviously did not. His neighbors are already eyeing the Aisir nam Breug, I'm told. If this Hay fellow had the stones to attempt to steal a march on them, and come to me in an effort to gain an advantage, then he fears someone else gaining what he covets. Ye'll be the answer to Dugald Kerr's prayers, Cousin. Now get ye into the Borders before there is bloodshed over the matter. I have only just gotten the lairds there settled down after years of running roughshod over my authority," the king said. "Return to Edinburgh on the morrow to fetch yer servant. Shut up yer house. Then go south, Fingal Stewart. Hopefully the lass will be pretty enough to please, but if she isn't, just remember that all cats look alike in the dark." And James Stewart laughed. "Bring her back to court when I have returned with my queen."

"Yer taking me from relative obscurity, gifting me with a wealthy wife, and giving me control of an asset that is valuable to you, and to Scotland. I will be a man of power, my lord," Fingal Stewart said quietly. "Other than my undying loyalty, what will ye require of me in return for this bounty?" His candid gaze met the king's eyes, and James Stewart laughed aloud.

"Yer a canny fellow, Cousin," he complimented his companion. "I will take half of the tolls ye collect from travelers, payable on Michaelmas each year in hard coin."

"One-third," Fingal Stewart dared to counter. "The pass must be maintained in good condition, and the laird I am certain supports his people with these monies. Remember I am a stranger coming at your behest to wed its heiress, and take control no matter whether the old laird welcomes me into their midst. Nothing must appear to change for the Kerrs of Brae Aisir other than a husband for the heiress. Remember, my lord, I have naught but my sword and yer word to recommend me. My purse is empty."

James Stewart nodded. He was known to be tightfisted, but he was also no fool. A third of the yearly tolls from this traverse was a third more than he had previously had.

He held out his hand to his cousin. "Agreed!" he said as they shook.

Lord Stewart rose from his chair, recognizing that he was now dismissed.

"Thank ye, my lord. My sword and my life are yers forever." He bowed low.

The king nodded his acknowledgment of the words, and with a wave of his hand he dismissed his cousin from his presence.

Fingal Stewart turned and left the privy chamber. He found Janet Munro awaiting him in the dim corridor, and he told her of what had transpired.

"Yer a man of property now," she said in a well-satisfied voice. So many royal mistresses enriched themselves and their families during their tenure. She had not, accepting only what was offered. She knew her parsimonious lover would see her and her child comfortably supported. She was satisfied now to have done something for the cousin she had always liked. He was a good man and deserved a bit of good luck.

Digging into her skirt pocket, she pulled out a small pouch. "Ye dinna have to tell me the condition of yer purse, Fin. And ye canna travel without coin. The king wanted ye to have this." Janet thrust the purse at him. "Yer men-at-arms are just paid for the year. Ye may retain them for yer own, but next Michaelmas ye must pay their wages yerself. Ye have a house in the town, gold in yer purse, a servant, and twelve men-at-arms. Ye will nae appear a poor man when ye come to Brae Aisir, *and* yer the king's own blood to boot." Then standing on her toes, she put her arms about him and kissed his cheek. "God bless ye, Cousin."

He returned her embrace. "Thank ye, Jan. I know 'tis ye who have brought me this good fortune. Should ye ever need me, ye have but to send for me," Fingal Stewart said. He suspected the gold in the purse she had given him was from her own small store.

"Come along now," she said briskly. "There is food in the hall, and I've found a place for ye to lay yer head this night."

He followed her and while he ate at a table far below the high board in the king's hall, he looked about him. The chamber was filled with the mighty. Before she left him to join her lover, Janet Munro pointed out the Earl of Huntly; the young Earl of Glenkirk; Lord Hume, who was now warden of the East March; the provost of Edinburgh, Lord Maxwell; and George Crichton, bishop of Dunkeld, among others. Fingal Stewart watched the panorama played out before him, listening to all the gossip spoken.

He was, he decided, glad to be a simple man.

When the evening grew late, Janet Munro came to him again and brought him to the stables where his horse had been taken. "Ye can sleep here, Cousin," she told him, "but be gone by first light. Yer men will join ye at yer house tomorrow before ye depart."

He thanked her a final time, noting she

did not reveal aloud to where he was traveling, for she was wary of being overheard. His mission was after all a clandestine one; a preemptive strike to be carried out before anyone could prevent it. He slept several hours before rising in the pale light of the predawn, saddling his stallion, and riding back to Edinburgh. It was a chilly ride beneath the light rain now falling.

His manservant, Archie, was awaiting him anxiously. There had been no need for him to go with his master the previous day, but he had been concerned when six men-at-arms had arrived with Lady Janet to conduct Lord Stewart to Linlithgow. "My lord!" The relief in Archie's voice was palpable. "Yer home safe."

"Pack up all our personal possessions, what few we have, Archie," Fingal Stewart said. "I'm to have a wife, and a great responsibility that goes with her."

"My lord?" Archie's plain face was puzzled.

His master laughed. "Is there something to eat?" he asked.

"I'm just back from the cookhouse, my lord. Aye, come into yer hall," his servant said. "I've fresh bread, hard-boiled eggs, a rasher of bacon."

"Then let's eat, man, and I'll tell ye all,"

Lord Stewart said.

They went into the small chamber that served as the house's hall. The fresh food was already upon the high board, for Archie had taken the chance his master would return sooner rather than later. He quickly served his lord, poured him a small goblet of watered wine, and was then waved to a place by his side. The two men ate silently, quickly, and as the last piece of bacon disappeared from the plate, Fingal Stewart spoke.

Fingal explained all to Archie, concluding, "So, Archie, we are leaving Edinburgh and settling down with a wife, and a real home, and probably a covey of bairns eventually. Do ye think yer ready for such an existence?" Lord Stewart chuckled.

"I am!" his manservant said without a moment's hesitation. " 'Tis a blessing, it is, my lord, to have been given such a bounty. We're not getting any younger, either of us."

As big as his master was, Archie was a wee bit of a man, short and wiry with stone gray hair and sharp blue eyes. His family had served the Stewarts of Torra for many years, and but for his master, he was alone in the world now.

"Perhaps we'll find ye a nice plump lass to warm yer bed on those cold border nights," Fin teased, and he laughed aloud.

Archie laughed with him. "Aye, my lord, 'twould please me greatly if we did."

"My cousin, Lady Janet, has given me a purse, and the king has supplied us with twelve men-at-arms to go with us. They will be here shortly to escort us into the Borders, Archie. Ye had best hurry and pack us up now," Fingal Stewart said with a smile. "Can we leave within an hour or two? And shall I send for Agent Boyle and rent the house?"

"Nay, keep the house empty for now, my lord. What if ye want to bring yer lady to court once we have a queen? There's never any room at court for unimportant folk."

"The king prefers Linlithgow Palace to Edinburgh Castle," his master replied. "But yer right. I should not be hasty. Still send for Boyle and see what he says. We'll need the house watched so nothing is stolen while I am in the Borders."

Archie hurried from the hall, and opening the front door of the house, gestured to one of the lads always about the small street. "Go and fetch Agent Boyle to Lord Stewart. He must come immediately," Archie said. "There's a copper in it for you when you return with him."

The boy pulled at his forelock and ran off.

The rain was beginning to fall more heavily. Archie then went about the business of packing up what they would take. Less than half an hour had passed when a hammering came upon the front door. Archie ran to open it, admitting the house agent. He flipped the lad his copper while ushering Boyle inside. He led the man to the hall where Lord Stewart was packing up his weapons.

"Boyle's here, my lord," he announced.

Fingal Stewart looked up, beckoning the man to a seat by the fire. "Sit down, Boyle," he said. "Sit down. Archie, a dram of whiskey for Master Boyle."

"Thank ye, my lord, thank ye. 'Tis damp outside." He accepted the dram cup, and swallowed down its contents. Then he looked to Lord Stewart. "How may I serve you, my lord?" he asked politely.

"I have to leave Edinburgh for some months," Lord Stewart began. "I will need you to find someone to watch over the house so it not be burgled. Someone reliable who will not sell off my few possessions while I am gone," he told the house agent.

"Ye don't want to rent, my lord?" Boyle inquired.

Fingal Stewart shook his head in the negative. "What if I return before I anticipate? If I have no house, where can I lay my head and stable my horses?"

"I was nae considering a rental to a family, my lord. Men of importance come to Edinburgh, wealthy merchants, those high up in the church, among others. They are nae asked to the castle. They do not choose to house themselves at some inn. Their stays are brief. A few days, a few weeks, a month. And they pay well for their privacy and the discretion that a house like this can provide them, my lord. They bring their own servants and require naught but a secure shelter."

"And how much commission would you want for providing such a service, Master Boyle?" Lord Stewart inquired.

"But ten percent of the rental fee, my lord," Boyle answered him.

"I will want a woman in to clean before any come, and after they go," Lord Stewart said. "And you will pay her from your ten percent for I have nae a doubt that you will also collect ten percent from your clients as well."

The house agent's eyebrows jumped with his surprise.

"How much will you charge per day?" Fingal asked, and when Boyle told him, he nodded. "Do not consider you can cheat me by paying me for four days when the guest remains seven," he warned. "I have eyes that will watch ye. I will expect a proper rendering of my account every other month. You may deliver it to Kira's bank in Goldsmith's Lane. They will be informed to expect it, and will advise me if they do not get it, Master Boyle. If this is satisfactory to you, I will allow you this rental."

"Will ye be visiting the town yerself, my lord?" the agent asked.

"I will send to you when I am and will expect the house available to me when I come," Lord Stewart said sternly. "I will attempt to give you enough notice that your clients not be inconvenienced by my coming. Is this agreeable to you?"

Master Boyle nodded. "Quite, my lord."

Both men stood up and shook hands.

"I am departing today," Lord Stewart said. "Archie will give ye a key."

The house agent bowed and exited the hall where Archie was waiting for him. The manservant handed Master Boyle two keys on an iron ring. "Front door, and door from the kitchen into the garden," he said. He opened the front door, ushering the man out.

Master Boyle hurried out, and down the

street to the Royal Mile, stepping aside as he came to the congested wider way to allow a party of mounted men-at-arms to enter the small lane. He stopped, watching to see what business they could possibly have on such an undistinguished lane. His bushy eyebrows jumped as they halted before Lord Stewart's stone house. He peered down the dim street to see the badges on their jacket arms. The bushy eyebrows jumped again as he recognized the king's mark.

Well, well, well, Master Boyle thought. *What brings the king's men here? And what business could they have with my client?* Was he being arrested? Was that his reason for leaving Edinburgh for several months? But then he considered that Lord Stewart was undoubtedly related to His Majesty and was probably being sent on an errand for his master. Thinking no more about it, he hurried on his way through the rainy morning.

The men-at-arms in the lane dismounted, one of them pounding on the door to the house. Archie answered the summons with a few pithy words. "Is this how ye ask to enter the dwelling of the king's cousin?" he demanded of them. "Wipe yer booted feet, my lads. Come into the hall and warm yourselves. His Lordship is waiting for ye."

The dozen men followed Archie, several of them chuckling at the feisty little man as they entered the chamber. It was hardly an impressive room, but they knew from a servant of the king's mistress that the man awaiting them was the king's own kin. They stood in respectful silence waiting for whatever instructions this lordling would give.

Lord Stewart looked up. It was time to face his future. He took a deep breath and, rising from his chair by the small hearth, greeted the men-at-arms. "Good morrow, lads. Warm yerselves by the fire. We are almost ready to depart. Do ye know where we are going?" Lord Stewart asked the men.

The soldiers murmured in the negative.

"Choose a leader from among ye," he told them. "I need one of ye in charge of the others. Be ready with yer choice when I return." Then he left the hall to find Archie, who was just finishing packing up their possessions on the second floor of the house.

"They're a rough-looking bunch," Archie said as Lord Stewart entered his bedchamber. "I wonder if they're to be trusted."

Fingal Stewart shrugged. "We'll see soon enough, won't we?" he replied. Seeing his traveling garments laid out for him, he quickly stripped off the clothing he had worn to Linlithgow along with his leather boots. "I slept in a stable last night," he said ruefully, sniffing the velvet doublet.

"It can be aired out," Archie responded pragmatically. "I'll pack it with some clove to overcome the scent of the king's barn. Ye'll not be wearing it until yer wedding day." He carefully folded the garment and placed it with a few nails of the spice with the other clothing already in his master's small trunk. Before closing the lid, Archie reverently laid his master's plaid on top. Its background was green with narrow bands of red and blue, and slightly wider bands of dark blue. It was the ancient family tartan.

Fingal Stewart pulled on a pair of sturdy dark brown woolen breeks over his heavy knitted stockings, yanked his boots back onto his big feet, and pushed his sgian dubh into the top of the right one. The weapon had a piece of green agate sunk into its top, and its scabbard had Lord Stewart's crest set in silver. He tucked his natural-colored linen shirt into the pants, fastened a leather belt about his waist, drew on a soft brown leather jerkin with buttons carved from stag horn, and picked up his dark woolen cloak. He looked to Archie. "Are we ready?" he asked his serving man.

Archie nodded. "The fires are all out in

the house except in the hall."

The two men left Lord Stewart's chamber and descended back down into the hall where the men-at-arms now stood about the fire getting the last bit of warmth they could before their long ride. Archie went immediately to the hearth and began extinguishing the low flames and coals with sand from a bucket set near the fireplace.

"Have ye chosen a captain from among yerselves?" Lord Stewart asked them.

A man stepped from among them. He was almost as tall as Fingal Stewart. His features were rough-hewn, his hair a red-brown, his eyes, which engaged the taller man's fearlessly, blue. He had a big nose that had obviously been broken once or twice. "I am Iver Leslie," he said. "The lads have chosen me." He gave a small but polite bow.

Lord Stewart nodded and offered his hand to Iver, who took it in a firm grasp and shook it. "You'll ride next to me," Fingal Stewart said. Then he brought Archie, who had completed putting out the fire, forward and introduced him. "This is Archie, my servant. Sometimes he will speak for me, so listen when he does, and obey him. He's a wee bit of a fellow, but be warned he's handy with both his fists and a knife."

Archie nodded towards the men-at-arms,

who nodded back. "There's a bit of whiskey left in the keg at the end of the hall," he said. "Drink it, or put it in yer flasks, while I get our horses, lads." He grinned as they made a beeline for the keg; all but Iver remained by Lord Stewart's side. Archie's wise eyes spoke their approval of Iver.

"I'll bring the beasts around to the front, my lord," he said. Then he hurried from the hall.

"Go and get some whiskey for yerself," Fingal Stewart said quietly.

"Thank you, my lord."

Iver quickly went down the hall, and seeing him, his men made way for him. He filled his flask and came back to stand by Lord Stewart's side. "May I ask where we are going, my lord? We were not told."

"We are traveling into the Borders to a place called Brae Aisir," Fingal Stewart said. "I'm being sent to wed the old laird's granddaughter, his only heir. The laird is Dugald Kerr, and with his English kin on the other side of the Cheviots, they control a passage through the hills called the Aisir nam Breug that for centuries has been used only for peaceful travel. King James wants to keep it that way. The laird's neighbors have of late been showing signs of impatience, for the lass will not choose a husband, and if Dugald Kerr should die too soon, there is no male heir to look after this valuable asset."

Iver nodded. "Aye, a lass canna guard such a treasure without a husband."

"Yer not from the Borders," Lord Stewart said.

"Nay, I come from a village near Aberdeen," Iver informed his new master.

"Good! Then ye'll have no loyalties but to me, and to the king," Fingal Stewart remarked. "Are any among yer lot borderers?"

"Nay, I know them all, my lord. They all come from Edinburgh or Perth or somewhere in between. None are from the Borders," Iver replied.

Lord Stewart nodded. "Tell them where we are going, and why. We are not invaders but the king's representatives. I expect good behavior. Any man who can't behave will face punishment at my own hand. I'm a fair man, and expect the truth from every mouth. I'll not punish a man for the truth, but if I catch him in a lie, 'twill go hard on him. Do ye understand, Iver?"

"I do, my lord, and I'll see the lads understand too. Might I ask if the laird is expecting us?"

"He is not, but the king believes he will welcome us nonetheless."

"The king would know," Iver replied pragmatically.

Archie returned. "I've got the horses, my lord."

Lord Stewart flung his cloak about his shoulders. Iver called to the men to come. Archie brought up the rear, and locked the house door behind him. He then climbed up onto his horse, taking the lead rein from the horse serving as a pack animal for them. The rain was falling steadily as they clattered down the lane and out onto the Royal Mile. The serving man hunched down. It was late summer, and while the rain wasn't cold as it might have been in another season, it was still uncomfortable. He hoped the weather would turn for the better by nightfall or at least on the morrow. It didn't.

They rode until it grew too dark to ride. There was no shelter but a grove of trees when they stopped. It was too wet to light a fire. They pulled oatcakes and dried meat from their pouches, washing them down with some of the contents from their flasks. The horses were left to browse in the nearby field while their riders huddled beneath the greenery with only their cloaks to keep the rain from them. The next day and night were no better. They avoided any villages along their way so as not to arouse curiosity.

"Yer captain has explained where we are going. A troop such as ours would cause chatter if we passed through them, or sheltered in them," Lord Stewart explained to his men on the second night. "We don't want the laird's neighbors becoming inquisitive. We'll reach Brae Aisir tomorrow sometime, if that is any comfort to you. It will be warm, and ye'll get some hot food in ye then."

They all held on to the thought that night, their backs against a rough stone wall, the thunder booming overhead, the lightning crackling about them. The horses had to be staked out and tied to prevent the frightened animals from fleeing. The rain poured down. The next morning, however, dawned bright and sunny. Lord Stewart instructed his men to change their shirts and stockings if they had the extra clothing. He was relieved that they all did. He wanted his men looking smart, not hangdog, when they entered Brae Aisir. The dry garments would help to raise their spirits.

Brae Aisir. He didn't know what to expect, but with its dark stone, a moat, a drawbridge that was up, and obviously fortified, it certainly wasn't what looked like a small keep upon a hillock. He wondered whether the king knew of this structure; perhaps he assumed that a prosperous border laird lived in a well-kept tower house or manor. Fingal Stewart was suddenly aware that the Aisir nam Breug was more important than just a traverse between England and Scotland. How had they managed to keep warring factions from using it? He obviously had a great deal to learn about his new responsibilities. He hoped old Dugald Kerr was up to teaching him. They had stopped to observe the keep.

Now Lord Stewart turned to Iver. "Send a man ahead to tell them I come for the laird on the king's business. We'll wait here until we are asked to proceed. I don't want the village below put into a panic fearing that we are raiders."

Iver gave a quick order, and a single man detached himself from the group, galloping down the hill, through the village, and up to the keep. He stopped before the raised drawbridge, and waited. Finally a wood shutter on a window to one side of the entry was flung back. A helmeted head appeared.

"What do ye want?" a voice shouted down to him.

"Messenger from Lord Stewart, who waits on the other side of the village. He comes to the laird bearing greetings and a message from King James. May he have permission to enter?"

"Wait!" the voice said, and the shutter slammed shut.

After several very long minutes the shutter banged open, and the voice called, "The laird bids your master come forth. He is welcome to Brae Aisir."

"Thank ye," the messenger said politely and, turning his mount, headed back down the hill, through the village, and up the hill on the other side. Behind him he heard the creaking of the drawbridge as it was being lowered. "Yer welcome to enter the keep, my lord," he told Fingal Stewart when he had reached the place where his party of horsemen awaited his return. "They were lowering the drawbridge as I returned to ye."

Lord Stewart turned to his men. "We will ride through the village sedately. These borderers are a prickly lot. I don't want anyone, child or creature, trampled with our coming. We are welcomed, and 'tis not a race." Then swinging about, he raised his hand and signaled his party forward.

Villagers going about their daily chores stopped to move from the road and stare at the riders. A fountain and well were in the center of the hamlet. Several women were there getting water. They turned to stare boldly at the strangers. One pretty young lass even smiled at the men-at-arms and was immediately smacked by an older woman, obviously her mother. There was a small chapel at the far end of the village that they passed as they began to ascend the far hill to the keep. A priest stood before the little church, watching them, unsmiling, as they passed him by.

Reaching the keep, they clattered across the wooden drawbridge. As they did, the iron portcullis was slowly raised so they might pass through into the keep's yard. Fingal looked carefully about him, drawing his mount to a halt. Within the walls was a large stone house with two towers, a stable, a well, and a barn. The courtyard was not cobbled but had an earth floor still muddy with several large puddles from the past days' rain. As he dismounted, a man hurried forth down the stairs from the house.

"My lord," he said with a bow. "I am Busby, the laird's majordomo. Ye are most welcome to Brae Aisir. The laird is waiting for ye in the hall. Yer men are welcome to enter as well. The hearths are blazing, for the day is cool despite the welcome sunshine. Summer is coming to an end, and I imagine yer travels have been wet." He led the visitor briskly up the steps, into the house, and down a broad passage into the great hall. "My lord, Lord Stewart," Busby said, bringing the visitor to his master.

Dugald Kerr stood up and held out his hand. The laird was tall, but not nearly as tall as the man before him. He had a full head of snow white hair, and his brown eyes carefully assessed Fingal Stewart. "Welcome to Brae Aisir, my lord. Sit down! Sit down!" He indicated a settle opposite his high-backed chair as he sat once more.

A servant hurried up, tray in hand, and offered a goblet of wine first to his master, then to his master's companion.

The laird raised his goblet. "The king!" he said.

Lord Stewart reciprocated. "The king!" he responded.

The two men drank in silence.

Then the laird said to his guest, "Yer messenger said ye come from the king with a message for me, my lord. Yer James Stewart's kinsman?"

"I am," Fingal replied. He reached his hand into his jerkin, and drew out the small rolled parchment he had been given to bring to the laird, handing it to him.

"Do ye know what is in this?" Dugald

Kerr asked candidly.

"I do, my lord," Fingal replied.

Nodding, Dugald Kerr broke the dark wax seal on the parchment and unrolled it. His sharp eyes scanned the writing, and then he looked up. "How did the king learn of my *difficulties?*" he asked.

"A man named Ewan Hay came to him with a story the king believed to be but a half-truth," Fingal said. "But learning of the Aisir nam Breug, the king became concerned for yer safety, the safety of yer granddaughter, and the safety of this traverse, my lord."

The laird nodded again. "And yer willing to wed my Maggie, my lord?"

"I do not believe that either of us has a choice in this matter," Fingal replied, "but I swear to you, my lord, I shall treat yer granddaughter honorably and fairly."

"Nay, neither ye nor I has a choice," the laird said. "But Maggie will be a different story altogether, sir. I dinna envy ye yer courting." And Dugald Kerr chuckled richly, his brown eyes dancing with amusement. " 'Twill be a rough wooing, I fear."

CHAPTER 3

As the laird enjoyed his mirth, Maggie Kerr entered the hall. "I am told we have a visitor, Grandsire," she said, coming forward.

Fingal Stewart watched her come. She was dressed in woolen breeks, boots, and an open-necked shirt. A wide leather belt encircled her waist. The skin of her neck and face was damp with obvious exertion. The lass was more than pretty, he realized, but the confident stride as she walked, the open curiosity in her hazel eyes, the set of her jaw, told him she would be neither biddable nor easy. He stood politely as she came forward.

"The king has sent ye a gift, lassie," the laird chortled. He was truly enjoying this.

"The king? A gift?" She looked genuinely puzzled. "The king has never set eyes upon me. Why would he send me a gift?"

"Ewan Hay went to visit His Majesty. He told him ye needed a husband, lass," the laird cackled. "And so the king has sent his own kinsman to wed ye." The laird waited for the outburst that was not long in coming.

"Ewan Hay told the king I needed a husband? Why would that pox-ridden donkey's ass do such a thing?" Then her eyes widened. "God's balls! He thought to steal Brae Aisir out from beneath us, Grandsire, didn't he? He thought the king would order me to wed him, the imbecile!" Then her eyes fixed themselves on her grandfather's companion. "Who are ye, sir?"

"Lord Fingal Stewart, madam," Fin answered her.

"And yer the king's kin sent to wed me?" she demanded.

"I am," he replied.

"And what, my lord, have ye done to win such a prize?" Maggie wanted to know.

"I have been loyal, madam. The Stewarts of Torra have always been loyal to the Stewart kings since the days of James the First. The king knows he may trust me to do as I have been bid," Fingal Stewart answered her in a hard voice.

"Torra? *Of the rock?*" Maggie was curious in spite of herself. "Where do ye come from, my lord?"

"Edinburgh, madam. We are the Stewarts

of Torra because our house sits below the castle rock itself," he told her.

"Ye have no lands then," she said scornfully.

"I have a house, a manservant, twelve men-at-arms gifted me by the king, some coin with Moses Kira, the banker, a modest purse of gold I've brought with me, and James Stewart's favor. Naught else," Fingal Stewart responded honestly.

Maggie had not expected a candid answer. She had never met a man before who was quite so direct. Usually men struggled to please her, to win her over — even that obnoxious simpleton Ewan Hay. "So ye've come to wed me for my wealth," she said, contempt tingeing her voice.

"I've come to wed ye because I have been ordered to it," he replied as insultingly.

"If ye think to wed me, my lord, ye will have to comply with the same rules all my other suitors have faced. And none has succeeded to date. I'll wed no man, particularly a stranger, whom I cannot respect. If ye can outrun me, outride me, and outfight me, I'll go to the altar willingly, but not otherwise."

"There's no choice here, lass," the laird told his granddaughter. "This man has been sent by the king, and I tell you truthfully that I am happy to see him. Ye'll wed him, and that's the end of it. Will ye let a man like Ewan Hay dispossess ye when I'm dead? Make no mistake, lassie, without a strong husband to follow in my path, our neighbors will be fighting ye and one another for control of the Aisir nam Breug."

"But Grandsire, if he does not compete against me, those same neighbors will rise up against the Kerrs for having imposed our conditions upon them, but not upon the king's kinsman," Maggie argued. "Ye swore before them that all suitors must conform."

"The lass is right," Fingal Stewart agreed. "If I am to have the respect of yer neighbors, my lord, I must accept the lady's challenge. 'Twill not be difficult to overcome her. I'm surprised this Hay couldn't."

Maggie suddenly grinned wickedly. "I can outrun, outride, and outfight *any* man in the Borders, my lord," she repeated, "and I will, I promise ye, outrun, outride, and outfight ye."

"I am not from the Borders," Lord Stewart reminded her with an answering grin.

"Ye can have yer contest, Maggie," her grandsire said, "but first I will have the marriage contract drawn up. Ye and Lord Stewart will sign it. When the contest is over, win or lose, ye must accept the marriage and have yer uncle bless it in the chapel."

She hesitated.

"Are ye afraid I'll beat ye?" Lord Stewart taunted her.

"I'm just concerned with having to live with a weakling," Maggie said sharply.

He laughed. "Madam, have ye ever been spanked?" he asked her.

She turned an outraged face to him. "Nay, never!"

"Ye will be, and soon, I have not a doubt," he told her.

"Lay a hand on me in anger, my lord, and I'll gut ye from stem to gudgeon," Maggie told him fiercely, her hand going to the dagger at her waist.

The laird's face grew grim at her combative words, but before he might admonish her, Lord Stewart laughed aloud.

"Marrying a stranger cannot be easy for either bride or groom, madam," he told her, grinning. "I can but hope this passion of yers extends to the marriage bed, for then we will suit admirably, and there will be no talk of murder, I promise ye."

Though Maggie was tall for a woman, he towered over her. She gasped and blushed at his blunt speech. No man had ever spoken so suggestively to her. For a moment she was at a loss for words. Then she said, "I'll sign the marriage contract, for in law that will make ye my husband. And I'm certain that will convince the greedier among our neighbors that the Aisir nam Breug's future ownership is settled. Particularly after they have met ye. Ye would appear to be reasonably intelligent and competent, my lord. But ye will nae bed me until ye have fulfilled my terms."

"Maggie!" Her grandfather almost shouted her name. "Ye cannot set the terms of this matter. The king has said ye will wed him, and ye will!"

"Aye, I will, Grandsire, but for the reasons earlier stated, he must best me," she replied. "The king said I must wed him — not lie with him."

"I will best ye, lassie," Fingal Stewart told her quietly. "Here's my hand on it." He held out his big hand to her, smiling.

She took his hand, watching almost mesmerized as his long thick fingers closed over her smaller hand, enclosing it completely as they shook. Then he shocked her by yanking her forward. An arm clamped about her waist, pulling her close against him. His chest was hard, and she could smell a mixture of male and the damp leather of his jerkin. A hand grasped her head, those same fingers wrapping themselves in her chestnut hair to hold her steady as his mouth descended upon hers in a fierce, quick kiss that left her breathless and gasping with surprise. He released her as quickly as he had taken her. Maggie stumbled back, but then, swiftly recovering, raised her hand to slap him.

The big hand sprang forth to wrap firmly about her wrist. "Nah, nah, lassie," he warned her softly. "I have the right now."

"Yer hurting me," Maggie said through clenched teeth, "and ye have no rights yet, my lord."

The laird watched the interaction between his granddaughter and Lord Stewart, fascinated. He would have to thank the king for sending him such a strong man to take on his responsibilities, not that he was quite ready yet to relinquish them. Fingal Stewart had a great deal to learn about the Aisir nam Breug. But he obviously was already skilled at handling a woman. Dugald Kerr chuckled.

"Are ye going to allow this ape to manhandle me, Grandsire?" Maggie demanded. She was utterly outraged. He had kissed her! Made her feel weak, and she wasn't weak. *She wasn't!* And her grandfather had done nothing to prevent it. Indeed, he had laughed.

"I'm going to call for David to come and meet Lord Stewart. I want yer marriage contract signed by the morrow. What date will ye fix for the challenge, lassie?"

"I'll sign the contract, for I have already given ye my word, but the challenge will have to wait, Grandsire. We are only just past Lammastide. We have late crops to harvest, and the fields must be opened for gleaning. When this is done, we will set a date, Grandsire," Maggie said.

"I am content with that," Lord Stewart quickly said, for he could see the laird was eager to have the matter settled and ended. "Send for the priest I saw in the village as we passed through, and let us make a beginning to it."

"Busby," the laird called. "Send for my brother to come to the keep immediately, and tell him to bring parchment and pen."

"I must go back to the yard, Grandsire," Maggie said. "I was training the new lads when I was told of Lord Stewart's arrival." Without waiting she made a quick curtsy to both men and hurried out of the hall.

"She trains the recruits?" Lord Stewart was surprised.

The laird nodded. "In archery, and other combat skills," he said. "Do ye now see why I have acquiesced to her demand that a husband be able to outrun, outride, and outfight her? She is beautiful, and she is clever, but she would rather be outdoors than in the hall. She has been that way since she was a wee lass. And from the moment I taught her how to use a bow, her pursuits were more those of a lad than of a lassie. She governs the house as well, for Grizel, her tiring woman, made her learn the things she must know to manage it. I pray God that you can overcome her, my lord, for Brae Aisir will be all the safer for an heir or two. I wish she were not so difficult, and I too old to control her."

Lord Stewart sat down again and sipped from his goblet. "She is a strong woman — she must be to survive here in the Borders," he began. "She has become formidable, I suspect, to protect ye and the Aisir nam Breug. The signing of the contracts on the morrow makes us legally man and wife. Beneath her brave heart and fierce will, yer granddaughter is still a woman. She knows she cannot escape the king's will, but she is afraid, though she would deny it. The moment my lips touched hers, I knew she had never been kissed. Let her have the time she needs to accustom herself to our marriage. Let us learn to know each other before I bed her. Ye need have no fear. I will beat her in whatever challenge she puts forth. And when I do, she will do her duty, for I know ye have raised her to accept her responsibilities."

"The king cannot possibly know the great favor he has done for us in sending ye here, Fingal Stewart," the laird said. Then his brown eyes twinkled mischievously. "How much is it costing Brae Aisir?" he asked.

Lord Stewart laughed. "I see my cousin's reputation extends into the depths of the Borders," he replied. "He wanted half of the yearly tolls paid each Michaelmas in coin. I argued for a third. When the contracts for our agreement reach me, I shall ask they be paid on St. Andrew's Day beginning next year. I believe that is fairer as I have no idea what ye collect, although judging from yer keep, I must assume it is a goodly sum."

"It is," the laird said, but gave no further details.

"Perhaps tomorrow the lady will ride out with me so I may see the pass," Lord Stewart suggested.

"Aye, before the winter comes there is much you will need to see and learn about Brae Aisir. And tomorrow I shall send one of my own men to the king with my thanks for sending ye. If ye wish to write to him, my messenger can take yer letter too."

Father David Kerr, robes swaying, hurried into the hall, his servant behind him carrying the priest's writing box. "What is so important that I must come posthaste, Dugald?" he asked his older brother. The priest's eyes went to Lord Stewart.

"This is Fingal Stewart, Brother. The king has sent his cousin, Lord Stewart of Torra, to wed with Maggie," the laird began. Then he went on to explain.

The priest listened, nodding as his elder brother spoke. When the laird had finished he said, " 'Tis as good a solution as any, Dugald." He held out his hand to Fingal. "Welcome to Brae Aisir, my lord." The two men shook. Then David Kerr looked back to the laird. "And what, pray, does my niece think of this? I saw her when I came into the courtyard working her lads hard. I think she is not pleased to be told what she must do."

"She will sign the marriage contract tomorrow when it is drawn and ready," the laird assured the priest.

"And the blessing?" the priest asked.

"He must fulfill the conditions any other suitor would before the blessing," Dugald Kerr said. "She is determined, and Lord Stewart says he can beat her fairly."

"You would let her have her way in her foolishness?" David Kerr asked Fingal.

He nodded in the affirmative. "Aye. She needs to feel she has some control over her life even if she doesn't. Some men might not care, but I want my wife to respect me. She will not if I cannot best her. And yer neighbors will not feel so slighted by this match when I do."

The priest looked thoughtful, and then replied, "Yer a clever fellow, my lord. And I think ye could be dangerous, given the opportunity. If yer willing to indulge the lass, then so be it. When will yer contest take place?"

"After the gleaning," Lord Stewart replied.

"Well, 'tis not so long to wait," the priest said. "I'm pleased to see yer a disciplined man."

"Remain here tonight, and draw up the contracts," the laird said. "I want them signed after morning Mass, Brother."

"Agreed!" David Kerr said. He turned to his assistant. "Tam, go and put my writing box in the laird's library. Then go home. I'll not need ye again till the morrow."

"Aye, Father David," the boy said, and hurried off to do as he had been bid.

A servant brought the priest a goblet of wine, and the three men sat talking before

93

one of the hall's two large hearths. Seeing them there as she came in, Maggie slipped up the stairs to her bedchamber where Grizel awaited. The serving woman had had her young mistress's tub set up, and the steam was rising from the hot water as Maggie entered the room.

"I didn't ask ye for a bath," the girl said.

"Yer not going down to the hall for the meal stinking of yer sweat like some man-at-arms," Grizel said firmly. "What will yer husband think of ye?"

"He's not my husband yet," Maggie said, irritated.

"He will be on the morrow," Grizel snapped back.

"Does everyone in Brae Aisir know my business now?" She pulled off her boots and garments impatiently.

"Fourteen mounted men ride through the village and up the hill to the keep, and ye think it will go unnoticed? Get in the tub before the water cools. A hall full of servants, and ye think no one is listening? This is the most exciting thing that has happened at Brae Aisir in years, lassie."

Maggie climbed into her tub. Taking up the washing rag, she soaped it and began to scrub herself vigorously. "The contract is to be signed tomorrow, and that's an end to it," she said. "I will have obeyed the king's command. There will be no bedding until he can prove himself worthy of me and earn my respect."

Grizel shook her head. "Yer the most stubborn lass in the Borders," she said.

"Aye, I am," Maggie agreed. "But if after proclaiming I should wed no man who could not outrun, outride, and outfight me, it would be Lord Stewart who would suffer if he did not rise to my challenge. There would be some like that boob Ewan Hay who would challenge his right to the Aisir nam Breug and cause a feud between the Kerrs and half a dozen clan families in the region. Let this *husband* the king has sent me prove to them all that he is worthy to take on this responsibility *and me.*"

"He's a big bonnie man," Grizel said. "He'll beat ye and show the others he can be the true master of Brae Aisir after yer grandfather relinquishes his authority."

"We'll see," Maggie replied to her tiring woman.

"Have ye decided when ye will issue the challenge?" Grizel asked her mistress.

"What? Has that information not been spread from the gossips in the hall yet?" Maggie teased her companion.

Grizel laughed. "Nay," she said.

"After the gleaning," Maggie told her, but she was already considering other ways to avoid doing what was really her duty. She would do this in her own time, not another's. She finished bathing, and after drying herself thoroughly, she dressed in the garments that Grizel had laid out for her — a plain gown of medium blue velvet brocade with a low square neckline, tight-fitting bodice, and tight sleeves. She wore her clan badge as a pendant on a gold chain. It showed the sun in its splendor with the motto *Sero sed servio,* meaning *Late, but in earnest.*

Grizel brushed out her mistress's beautiful warm brown hair. Then she set a French hood with a short trailing veil that fell just as far as Maggie's shoulders. The hood had a carefully pleated linen edge. "Put on yer slippers and yer ready to go down," Grizel said. "Ye look respectable and like a young lady should now."

"He wouldn't care what I looked like," Maggie said. "The Stewarts of Torra do their duty by the king, he told me. He's marrying me because the king said so and for no other reason, Grizel. He was insulting."

"It's yer own fault," Grizel told her bluntly. "Ye refused to get to know any of the marriageable men in the vicinity. Yer heart is nae engaged, lassie, so what does it matter whom ye wed now? Yer grandfather is sixty-three. He could wait no longer for ye to settle on a husband, especially as ye had no intention of doing so."

"But I can take care of the Aisir nam Breug, Grizel," Maggie said. "I don't need a husband to do it for me. Why do ye think I learned to ride, to run, to fight, to do accounts? It was so I could take over for Grandsire one day."

"And after ye?" Grizel said. "Who would care for the Aisir nam Breug after ye? Do ye think ye'll live forever, lassie? Ye need a husband, and bairns to follow ye."

Maggie sighed. "I know," she admitted. "I had just hoped to have more time."

"Yer seventeen, lassie," Grizel reminded her.

"Only last April," Maggie said.

"Yer mother birthed ye when she was sixteen," Grizel replied.

"And died in the process," Maggie answered.

"She was a sweet lass, but English, and weak," Grizel remarked. "Now get ye down to the hall, lassie. Ye know how yer grandsire dislikes it when yer late."

Maggie nodded, then hurried from her

bedchamber. In the hall she found her grandsire, the priest, and Lord Stewart much as she had left them, talking by the hearth.

She silently signaled Busby. "Is the supper ready?"

"It is, mistress. Shall I have it brought?"

"Aye. I imagine our guest is hungry at this point, and the rest in the hall as well. Was Cook able to find enough to feed the extra mouths?"

"She's using the extra bread she had, added more vegetables to the pottage, and sent her lad to fetch a new wheel of cheese to cut for the trestles," Busby informed his young mistress. "There'll be cold meats for the high board as well."

At a nod from Busby, the servants hurried from the hall to quickly return with the meal. Wooden bowls were set before each man at the trestles below the high board. They were filled by those same servants with a pottage of carrots, onions, leeks, and rabbit in a thick gravy. Bread and cheese were put on each table, and the tankards were filled with ale.

"My lords," Maggie said to the three men by the fire, "come to table." She ascended to the high board and seated herself in her place next to her grandfather's high-backed chair. Pewter plates, spoons, and silver goblets had been laid at the four places for the diners. There were bread, cheese, and a platter of cold meats along with the pottage, the main meal having been served hours earlier. Wine was poured into the goblets.

Lord Stewart looked about the hall as he ate. The chamber would be considered small by some; yet it was far larger than the hall in his house. It had two hearths, and four tall arched glass windows, two on each side of the room. It had a stone floor. A large tapestry hung behind the high board. Flag staffs with hanging battle flags had been set into the stone walls on the window sides of the hall, which had an arched roof with carved and painted beams. The room easily held five trestles and their benches. They were filled tonight. The chamber gave the appearance of prosperity not always seen in some halls.

And when he had ridden through the village earlier, it had looked comfortable as well. The cottages were well cared for, unlike in many villages. Their slate roofs were in good repair. He had seen no broken windows, and the doors were actually whitewashed. There was a large round fountain with a Celtic cross in the village's square. He had seen no garbage in the street, and the people appeared well fed. Brae Aisir was unique in that.

Maggie watched Lord Stewart from beneath her lowered lashes. What was he thinking? she wondered.

"I want ye to take Lord Stewart through the Aisir nam Breug tomorrow," the laird said. "Not all the way, just a half-day's ride, lassie. Explain to him how the defenses work. Don't go over the border, however. No need for the Netherdale Kerrs to know ye have a husband yet. We'll talk with them before the snows fall, or in the spring."

Maggie nodded. "I agree," she said. She turned to Fingal Stewart. "Their former patriarch, Edward Kerr, who was also my grandfather, thought I should wed one of my English cousins. I would not, for an English master at this end of the Aisir nam Breug would have been unsuitable. His loyalties would have been to whichever English king was in power, and not to our King James. And if the English controlled both ends of the pass, they might be cajoled into violating our long-held principles of only peaceful traverse. My mother was a Netherdale Kerr, but she was fragile and no Scot. I am a Scot, my lord, and I am not fragile. I am strong," Maggie said proudly.

Strong, proud, and beautiful, Fingal Stewart thought as she spoke. What a wife she was going to be! "I will be honored to be your husband, madam," he told her.

Maggie colored, her cheeks taking on a most becoming shade of pale rose. She dipped her head in silent response to his compliment, and reaching for her goblet, sipped her wine. Then she began to eat again with good appetite, he noted.

"She is not used to being courted," Father David Kerr said softly.

"I am surprised she is not wed," Lord Stewart responded in equally low tones.

"Her reputation is an honest one, my lord," the priest answered. "She is as fleet of foot as a deer being pursued by a pack of hounds. She rides astride, and like a demon."

"What is her weapon?" Lord Stewart asked.

"What isn't her weapon, although she will battle you with a claymore. She is an excellent archer. She can use a lance astride as well as any knight. She is skilled in hand-to-hand combat. To be candid with ye, my lord, my grandniece scares the very devil out of those who know her. Especially the young men, which is why none but Hay's fool of a younger brother attempted to meet her challenge. She was a-horse before the lad had even finished their footrace and was back in the keep courtyard, her ride finished as he sat with bloodied feet complaining. He gave up then. Lord Hay held no animosity towards the Kerrs. He had warned his sibling against making an attempt to vanquish Maggie."

"So that's why he went sub rosa to the king," Lord Stewart said aloud. "His pride had been badly damaged. He hoped James would hand over to him what he could not fairly win." Fingal Stewart laughed. "He misjudged my cousin badly."

"Could the king not have made a similar arrangement with the Hays as he made with ye?" the priest asked.

"Nay. Ye borderers are a fierce lot," Lord Stewart said with a smile. "Did he not spend some months subduing your earls? The king trusts few men, good Priest."

"But he trusts ye," David Kerr said. "Yer his blood."

"Even blood cannot always be counted upon," Fingal Stewart said wisely. "I am an exception not just because of my blood tie to the king, but my maternal grandmother was sister to the grandfather of the king's current mistress, Janet Munro. So the king and I are doubly bound. It was Janet Munro who informed the king of my existence, and how the Stewarts of Torra have never betrayed their kings. Until that day, the king had no knowledge of me at all despite our blood tie."

"I have heard stories both positive and negative about the king," Father David replied. "Yer tale is most interesting, my lord. It is a good thing that James Stewart acknowledges yer kinship, but also a good thing that ye have never been involved in any of the conspiracies that have surrounded him since his unfortunate childhood."

"I am six years the king's senior," Lord Stewart said.

"Then ye are thirty years of age, or thereabouts," the priest noted.

"Thereabouts," Lord Stewart agreed.

"Yer late to wed, or have ye been wed before?" the priest inquired.

"I have not been wed prior, nor to my knowledge do I have any bastards, and while I have known several women, I could not afford to keep a mistress," Lord Stewart said. "Is there anything else ye would know, good Father?"

The priest chuckled. "Ye understand why I ask, my lord. Ye are unknown to us, but ye come with written instructions from the king to wed our heiress. We cannot refuse the king's command, but we would know the kind of man into whose keeping we are placing our Maggie. One day when ye give yer daughter in marriage, ye will remember this day and understand."

"I descend from King Robert the Third through his murdered son, David, who got a son on his mistress, Maire Drummond. When the first James Stewart returned from an eighteen-year exile in England, his nephew came to pledge his undying loyalty. In return that king saw his nephew was permitted to use the surname Stewart; and he gave him a stone house with a fine slate roof below Edinburgh Castle, which is how we became the Stewarts of Torra. When the first James was foully murdered, that same nephew was one of the men who got the queen to safety and saw her son secured upon his throne. Since that day we Stewarts of Torra have never deviated in our loyalty," Fingal told the priest.

"We have never had the authority or the wealth to be involved in the battles to control the boy kings James the Second and James the Third. Nor did we take sides when the fourth James saw his father overthrown. We have simply remained loyal to the Stewart kings in power in any way we might. We have never broken faith with our kinsmen. So when our king told me to wed the heiress to Brae Aisir, I could give but one answer. Aye, my lord. My family's motto is *Ever faithful*. Our clan badge is a greyhound lodged in front of a crown proper. Is there anything else you need to know, Priest?"

"Ye have no siblings?"

"Nay. My father was content when I was born that he had a son. He had thought his line to die with him, for he was not a rich man and had not wanted to take a wife to share his poverty. He wed my mother, the orphaned kin of a friend, to keep her safe. She was sixteen and he past fifty when I was born. But he loved her, and she him. She died when I was ten, and my father just a few years ago."

"He would have been very old," Father David said.

Fingal chuckled. "He was eighty and had a strong constitution."

"Now I know what ye can tell me, my lord. The rest I shall learn as I come to know ye better. My brother, the laird, will not be unhappy with what you have told me."

Maggie had listened as Fingal had spoken to her great-uncle. His family might have had no wealth, but it would seem to be respectable with good clan connections — Munros, Drummonds, and Stewarts. She snuck a quick look at him from beneath her lashes. He was fair to her eye with his long face and shock of short, coal black hair. And his form was strongly built, and well muscled. She was tall for a woman, but he had topped her by at least half a foot. Could he overcome her fairly in the challenge? Would she let him? Or would she beat him as she would any man who attempted to best her?

Only time would tell, and Maggie needed to get to know Fingal Stewart better.

The following day they signed the marriage contracts drawn up by Father David, then met in the courtyard of the keep. They would ride with several men-at-arms, and she would show him the Aisir nam Breug. A late-August sun shone down on them, and above the skies were clear blue. They rode down the hill and through the village of Brae Aisir. A half mile from the village, Maggie turned her horse to the right, and Fin realized they were on a narrow and very ancient paved stone road. He was surprised when the hills suddenly rose up around them.

Seeing the look on his face Maggie said, "Aye, it comes upon ye suddenly, doesn't it.

This is the beginning of it. Our part runs for just over fifteen miles before the border is reached, and ye can cross into England."

"How do ye know when ye've reach the border?" he asked her.

"There is a cairn of stones topped by an iron thistle. A few feet farther on the other side of the pass is a second cairn of stones topped by a rose. Pass by it going south, and yer in England. Pass by our cairn going north and yer in Scotland. 'Tis that simple, my lord," Maggie explained patiently.

"I can see the road is too narrow for an army or group of raiders to travel with any urgency," Fingal Stewart noted, "but do ye have any defenses at all?"

Maggie smiled mischievously. "Look up and about ye, my lord."

He did, and it was then he saw the low stone watchtowers set at intervals, and carefully staggered on both sides of the pass. Lord Stewart was impressed.

"We keep three men in each tower," Maggie told him. "In case of an emergency, one man is sent to Brae Aisir or Netherdale, whichever is closer, to give the alarm."

"Yer English kin keep faith with ye first?"

"As we keep faith with them," Maggie replied. "The welfare of our folk is paramount for us all. Without the tolls we collect, how could we care for our people? We are not disloyal to our kings, and the pass has in its time prevented a tragedy or two because it has been a safe traverse through the Borders when there was no other way."

He nodded. It had all been carefully thought out, and it had been done several centuries ago. He was astounded that the Kerrs had been able to keep the Aisir nam Breug neutral and free of strife for all these years. Would he be able to successfully carry on the tradition? And what would the English Kerrs think of a Stewart marrying the last of the Brae Aisir Kerrs? They traveled that day to the border and back. And in the weeks to come Fingal Stewart took several of his men and rode the pass himself, familiarizing himself with the landscape, the watchtowers, the road itself.

August and September were over. The fields had been completely harvested, and the villagers were allowed to glean in them, gathering up what remained of the crops for their own families. The hillsides were bright with their autumn colors. One evening as October began, Dugald Kerr spoke to his granddaughter.

"It is time for ye to set the date of the marriage challenge," he said to Maggie.

"Och, Grandsire, we must bring the cattle

and sheep from the summer pastures first," Maggie said. "I have no time for racing now. Just yesterday one of the shepherds thought he heard a wolf in the far hills. I'll not lose good livestock to those beasties."

"I agree with her," Fingal Stewart said quietly.

The laird and his brother looked at each other. Finally Dugald Kerr said, "Well, 'twill not take long, and as yer already legally man and wife I suppose a few more days cannot matter." And the priest nodded in agreement.

So the sheep and the cattle were brought down from their summer pastures to browse in the fields near the keep during the day, and be penned safely within the village with their dogs at night. Again the laird asked his granddaughter to set the date for the challenge between her and Lord Stewart. But Maggie demurred a third time.

"Grandsire, we have not filled the larder with enough meat to get through the winter," she said in reasonable tones. "How can I rest and take my own pleasure if I permit this keep to go hungry come the snows?"

"I agree," Fingal Stewart murmured. "I commend your constancy to duty, madam. We will hunt together every day until we have enough meat to sustain us in the months ahead." He smiled pleasantly at her. "And then I will meet your challenge so our union may be blessed. The winter is as good a time as any to make an heir for Brae Aisir."

The old laird and the priest both chuckled at this, for Maggie's face had taken on a look of annoyance at Fingal Stewart's words.

"An excellent plan," Dugald Kerr said. "I'd like to be holding my great-grandson in my arms by this time next year," he said.

"And I'd like to be alive to baptize the bairn," Father David said.

Maggie's temper exploded. "I'll not be thought of as some damned broodmare to be bred for fresh stock," she told them.

" 'Tis yer duty, lassie," her grandfather told her. "Yer duty to Brae Aisir."

"I know my duty to Brae Aisir," Maggie said fiercely. "I have done that duty since I was a wee lass, Grandsire."

"Aye," he replied. "Ye've done duty by this family, and ye've done it well, but yer the last of us now, lassie, and yer duty is to give us a son. Ye've been given a good man for a husband. Now let him get a child on ye for Brae Aisir."

She ran from the hall, shocked by his words. Yet why should she be shocked? Her grandfather had only spoken the truth to her, and Maggie knew it. But still, to give up her authority to a stranger; to be nothing more than a creature to be bred? She did not know if she could bear it. She was close to tears. And then as she stood in the dimness of the corridor outside the hall, an arm went around her. Maggie stiffened her spine.

"He is eager to see an heir," Fin said quietly.

"Are ye?" The arm about her was more comforting than constraining.

"Aye, but not until yer content with this," Fin told her.

"Do ye want to bed me because ye must?" she asked.

He laughed softly, the warm breath soft against her neck as he bent down so only she might hear him. "I know ye have a mirror," he said. "Yer beautiful, lass."

"So bedding me will not prove too onerous a duty because I am beautiful," Maggie said testily.

"Lass, we are already wed by royal command. We must bed each other eventually. Am I to be distained because I appreciate that yer fair of face and form? As I come to know ye, I find that I like ye, Maggie Kerr. I admire yer honor and faithfulness to duty.

Set the date for yer challenge so Father David may bless our union," Fin said.

"Ye think ye can beat me?" Her tone was irritable.

"No one remains a champion forever, lass, and I am the man who will defeat ye," he said with surety. "Why are ye afraid of that?"

It had been comfortable leaning back against him, but now Maggie pulled away. She pushed his arm from her waist, pivoting about as she did. "I am Mad Maggie Kerr of Brae Aisir, and I fear no man," she said. "But before I set the date for this contest between us, the larder will be filled with meat. When that is done, I will set the time for our contest; ye have my word on it." She spit into her right hand and held it out to him.

He was surprised by the gesture, for it was not a woman's, but he spit into his right hand in return and shook her hand. "Done, madam, and done again!" he said.

Her gaze met his. "Yer a puzzlement to me, Fingal Stewart," she told him.

"Why?" he asked her. He puzzled her? 'Twas interesting, Lord Stewart thought.

"I am used to the society of men, but I have never known a man with such patience as ye have," she admitted. "Ye could lure a doe onto the spit."

"Is that why ye work at trying my patience, lass?" he queried, a small smile touching his mouth.

Maggie laughed. It was a loud sound, and filled with genuine amusement. "If there is a limit to yer patience, my lord, I have yet to find it," she admitted.

"There is a limit," he warned her. "But if I am indeed to lure the doe onto my spit, then I must exhibit great forebearance else it flee me into the hills."

"I will not run," she told him, blushing at the innuendo. I will leave ye now, my lord. We must be up and away before the dawn if tomorrow's hunt is to be successful."

He bowed to her. "Good night then, lass," he said. "I'll be up on time."

Maggie picked up her skirts and ran up the narrow stone stairs. She sensed he wanted to follow, but he did not, nor did she look back. He did puzzle her. If he was not an intimate part of the king's coterie, then what was he? He had been very candid with Father David about his past. And he had been equally candid with her. How had he lived? If he hired out his sword, where had he fought, and for whom? In France? She wanted to know more, but would her curiosity ever be satisfied? Or would she have to accept Fingal Stewart for what she saw, and what he had told her? Was there even more?

She thought there might be, but perhaps he needed to be more certain of her before he would tell her. Had the king investigated his kinsman, or had he just accepted the suggestion and the word of his mistress, who would, of course, want to aid her cousin?

"So," Grizel said when Maggie had closed her bedchamber door behind her, "yer grandfather is pressing ye again, or so says the gossip from the hall."

Maggie smiled. "First we fill the larder for winter," she replied.

"And after that?" Grizel asked, her brown eyes curious.

"I've given my word to set the date then for the contest between us," Maggie said.

"I know yer word is good." Grizel nodded. "Well, perhaps we'll have an early snow, and ye won't be able to settle the matter till spring."

Maggie laughed as she stripped off her garments. "I'm afraid Grandsire won't wait that long. I've been told he would hold his great-grandson in his arms by next autumn. And the priest concurred."

"I'll wager ye didn't like being told that," Grizel said as she shook out her young

114

mistress's gown, and hung it in the wardrobe.

Maggie sighed. "They're right, Grizel, although I will deny it, should you repeat my words. Lord Stewart seems to be a strong man, and he will hold the Aisir nam Breug as well as any Kerr before him. I can advise him until he is more certain of himself, but the truth is, other than keeping the accounts, my duty is to give Brae Aisir an heir."

"There is bound to be trouble when the Netherdale Kerrs learn ye've wed," Grizel said. "Lord Edmund has not been unhappy that ye've turned away all possible suitors."

"Edmund Kerr cannot believe that the English could manage the Aisir nam Breug alone. They control but eight miles of it to our fifteen. Those fifteen are Scots soil, not English. This cannot be Berwick all over again with the two sides wrangling over it. The pass would be useless then," Maggie pointed out.

"I think Lord Edmund hoped to wed ye himself," Grizel put forth. "He's put two wives in the ground already, but has been slow to seek another."

"He has nine sons, which should be enough for any man, and half a dozen are already wed with bairns of their own. Not to mention the bastards he sired on both sides of the border. The Netherdale Kerrs have no lack of heirs," Maggie remarked. "Besides, he's my uncle and close to fifty if he is a day. The rumors say he has a very devoted and jealous mistress. There is even speculation that she hurried his last wife to her death in order to become Lord Edmund's third wife. He can't seriously have any expectations of wedding me, and if he does, it is simply to get his hands on the entire Aisir nam Breug. I honestly doubt he could outrun, outride, and outfight me, Grizel." Now in her nightgown, Maggie undid her plait and began brushing out her long chestnut brown hair.

"Will ye hunt tomorrow?" Grizel asked her mistress as she finished putting away all of her garments. She picked up the girl's boots and polished the dust from them with a cloth she pulled from her skirt pocket.

"Aye, I want the larder filled by Martinmas," Maggie said. "I'll take us to that wee loch near the pass entrance tomorrow early. There have been geese overnight there.

"We'll catch them as they rise from the water to begin their southward flight. If everyone's arrow rings true, we will come back with a dozen or more."

"Lord Stewart's Archie says the villagers

have seen a boar in the wood lately," Grizel told her mistress.

"I had heard," Maggie answered. "Aye, I'd like to get that boar. If he's young, he'll be tender and make a fine feast on Christ's Mass day." She climbed into her bed, drawing the down coverlet up and settling back into her pillows. "I love hunting in the autumn the best," she said. "Good night, Grizel."

"Good night, my lady," the tiring woman answered as she departed her mistress's bedchamber.

As the door clicked shut behind Grizel, Maggie closed her eyes. Tomorrow would be a wonderful day, she decided. She would show Fingal Stewart that she was more than just a female upon whom he would breed up sons. She would take more game than he did, if only to irritate him. He said his patience had limits. She wondered whether that patience would come to an end if she pricked his pride hard enough. With a smile upon her face, Mad Maggie Kerr fell into a sound and most contented sleep.

CHAPTER 4

She was up before Grizel even came to awaken her the following morning. She could see the dark sky with a narrow shaft of waning moon through the half-open wood shutter. Maggie lay briefly enjoying a few last minutes of warmth before throwing her coverlet back and getting up from the bed. Pulling the night jar from beneath the bed she peed, leaving it for Grizel to empty. Then, going to her small hearth, she added some bits of kindling, coaxing her fire up from the dark red coals. As it lit, she added more wood, then pulled the ceramic pitcher from the coals where it had sat the night long keeping the water in it warm.

Maggie stripped off her simple white cotton nightgown. Pouring some water into a pewter basin, she picked up the washing rag, soaped it with a sliver of soap that had the fragrance of woodbine, and washed herself thoroughly. Then, using her most prized possession, a small brush with short, hard boar's bristles set into a piece of carved horn, Maggie scrubbed her teeth. Her ablutions concluded, she opened the trunk at the foot of her bed and drew out a cotton chemise that came only to her midthighs. It was lined in rabbit's fur. Putting it on, she added a white linen shirt over it, lacing it up. Next she pulled on a pair of woolen stockings and dark woolen breeks, which she secured with a wide belt. Next came a fur-lined soft doeskin jerkin and her leather boots.

As Maggie sat back down upon her bed to brush out her long hair and braid it into its single plait, Grizel came into the chamber. "Good morrow," Maggie said cheerfully, affixing a small bit of scarlet ribbon to hold her braid.

"Ye should have waited," Grizel said.

"I awoke and couldn't lie there. Besides, I'll want to eat before we go."

"I'll go fetch something," Grizel said.

"Nay, I'll go to the kitchens," Maggie said as she hurried from her bedchamber. She ran down the stairs to the hall and from there down another short flight of steps to the warm kitchens, where the cook and her helpers were busy at work. To her surprise Lord Stewart was already there, seated at the table where the cook and her staff usually sat.

"Good morrow, my lord," Maggie greeted him as she sat down. Immediately a bowl of oat porridge was put before her. Maggie spooned a bit of honey into it and poured in some heavy golden cream before she began to eat enthusiastically.

"Yer up early," he remarked.

"We're hunting," she said matter-of-factly. "The beasties are up too, my lord."

The cook plunked a hot cottage loaf on a wooden board between them with a knife and a tub of butter. She cut two wedges, handing them each one.

"Have ye some hard-boiled eggs and bread for us to take?" Maggie asked the cook.

"Aye, my lady, and a bit of cheese and apples as well," the cook answered her. "Iver took it to pack up in the saddlebags."

"Iver?" Maggie looked confused.

"My captain," Lord Stewart said as he smeared butter across his bread with his big thumb.

"Oh, aye," Maggie said, remembering. "We've got to do something more to integrate your men with our men, my lord. They have kept apart from each other since ye arrived."

"Aye," he agreed. " 'Tis a knotty situation, madam, but it must be corrected. The captain of this keep's men-at-arms is not a young man, but I have already seen he has earned his position by being good at what he does. Would he consider accepting Iver as his second in command? Or does he have a man in that position already?"

"Nay, he does not," Maggie said. "The problem for Clennon Kerr is that he is related to almost every family in Brae Aisir. He has several nephews among his men. They are his two sisters' sons. How can he choose from between not just them but the rest of the men without offending someone among his kinsmen? So he has kept the authority to himself. I will speak with my grandfather when we have returned from the hunt today. If it pleases him to do so, he will appoint your man, Iver, to be Clennon Kerr's second in command. Will that suit you, my lord?"

"It will," Lord Stewart replied. Then he turned and looked sternly at the cook and her helpers. "There will be no gossip should you have overheard our conversation. If word gets out before the laird is consulted, and Clennon Kerr is consulted, I will know where to lay the blame. My justice will be harsh and swift. Do ye all understand me?"

The cook nodded. "I'll keep all here as silent as the grave," she promised.

He nodded, satisfied, and gave her a smile of approval.

They had finished their meal and now walked upstairs to the hall where those accompanying them were gathering. Some of the men were eating oatcakes and drinking from their flasks. It was the kind of meal they could finish a-horse. Seeing Lord Stewart and his companion, Iver signaled the men to move out into the courtyard.

It was still dark outside, but the edges of the sky were showing signs of light as they mounted up. With Maggie and Fingal Stewart leading them, they exited forth from the keep's courtyard. The horses' hooves made a soft *clop clop* as they went. A pack of dogs ran by their side, yapping softly.

"Where are we going?" he asked her.

"There's a small water near the pass entrance. The geese overnight there on their way south this time of year. They fly at dawn. We'll be there in time," Maggie assured him. "And there's a boar that has been seen in the the nearby wood."

They reached their destination. The sky above them was considerably lighter than it had been when they left the keep. Tethering their horses, they crept through the underbrush to see a large flock of birds floating upon the placid water. They could hear the soft cackle of bird talk as they prepared their bows, carefully notching their arrows, and then waiting patiently for the moment when the birds would instinctively fly.

The horizon began to show signs of blazing color. The scarlet and gold spread out along the edges of the sky. And then as the sun burst forth over the purview of the blue, the flock of geese rose up from the water, their cackling and the sound of their flapping wings making a great noise. The hunters stood up, and the arrows from their bows being loosed flew towards the birds. Some quicker than others rearmed and shot a second time. A rain of geese fell into the water while the birds that had escaped flew up and southward.

"Loose the dogs!" Maggie cried.

The water dogs among the pack dashed into the small pond, swimming towards the dead geese. Finally when all the birds had been gathered up and brought ashore, Maggie instructed one of the younger men among them to take them immediately back to the keep, where they would be hung head down in the winter larder until they would be needed for a meal. They counted twenty-seven geese among their kill.

" 'Twas nicely done," Fingal Stewart said to Maggie.

"If I couldn't outthink a goose, what kind of a chatelaine would I be?" she asked him, grinning broadly.

"Still a beautiful one," he told her, grinning back as she colored prettily.

"Now we have a boar to find," Maggie replied, quickly changing the subject. "He'll be more difficult, but if he's young, not so wily as an older boar."

They rode away from the little water now devoid of birds, directing their horses' steps towards a woodland bordering the village. But though they hunted the morning long, they could find no game at all. Just before dark, they took a young stag. Maggie was not at all satisfied. She wanted that boar.

"We'll hunt every day until we find him," she said to Lord Stewart.

They returned to the keep where the stag was butchered and hung in the winter larder, which was a little more than half full. If the weather remained decent, they should be able to fill it by month's end, for there was plenty of game in the vicinity, Fingal Stewart thought to himself. Though they had missed the main meal of the day, the cook had provided them with trenchers filled with hot lamb stew that they consumed immediately. Afterwards Maggie spoke with her grandfather, Lord Stewart by her side.

She explained to the laird the necessity of combining the keep's men-at-arms with the men who had come with Fingal Stewart. "The two groups should be blended into one underneath the command of Clennon Kerr, Grandsire. But since our captain has never been able to choose a second in command, I would suggest that Lord Stewart's captain, Iver Leslie, fill that position. Clennon Kerr must be consulted, of course, but it needs to be done sooner than later," Maggie told her grandfather.

"Aye," the old man agreed. "It will also help my new grandson to be accepted by all here if we make the two groups one."

"Your new grandson?" Maggie said sharply.

"He's yer legal husband, lassie, which makes him my grandson," the laird answered her pleasantly. He signaled to Busby, and when he had come to his master's side, the laird said, "Fetch Clennon Kerr to me."

"Aye, my lord," the majordomo said, hurrying off.

Several minutes passed in silence, and then Clennon Kerr came bowing to the laird, to Lord Stewart, and to Maggie. "Ye

125

wish to see me, my lord?"

The laird explained, and when he had finished, his captain nodded in agreement.

"Aye, my lord, 'twill suit me well. I have watched Iver Leslie in the weeks he has been here. He is a disciplined soldier," Clennon Kerr replied. "And now that ye have made this decision, my sisters will have to cease nagging at me to promote this relation or that," he chuckled. "And no one can claim I have favored my close kin over any other."

"Busby!" the laird called, and when Busby came, he was sent for Iver Leslie.

Iver, who had been dicing with his Edinburgh companions at the end of the hall, gathered up his small winnings and hurried to the side of the laird of Brae Aisir. "Ye wished to see me, my lord?" he asked, bowing politely and casting a quick look at Lord Stewart.

"With yer master's permission, and that of my own captain, Clennon Kerr, I have decided to make ye second in command of the keep's men-at-arms."

Iver's face showed genuine surprise. "My lord, surely one of yer own could fill this position better than I," he said. "I am honored, and will of course accept, but I should not take another's legitimate place."

"I am related to everyone in Brae Aisir," Clennon Kerr told Iver. "How can I pick one of my relations over another without causing offense? The laird has made his decision, and I am frankly relieved." He held out his big hand to Iver Leslie, whose equally large hand clasped it in friendship.

"Busby!" the laird called. "Drams of whiskey all around." Then he looked at the two soldiers. " 'Tis settled then. The decision was mine, Clennon Kerr. Yer sisters cannot blame ye, and the rest of yer kin will be relieved, I'm thinking."

Busby himself brought the tray with the dram cups of whiskey. A health was drunk to the laird's wisdom. The matter was settled but for one thing.

Going to stand at his place at the high board, the laird called out, "Hear me all within this hall and the sound of my voice. I have appointed Iver Leslie to be the keep's second in command after Captain Clennon Kerr. Now let's have a round of ale to celebrate, laddies."

And the serving men were at the trestles filling the tankards. A health was drunk to the two captains. Then the hall settled back down into its usual evening routine. The laird questioned his granddaughter as to the hunt that day and the state of the larder.

"The larder is filling nicely. A few more weeks and we'll have it done," Maggie said. "By the beginning of December for certain, Grandsire."

"Set the date for yer contest, then, for December," Dugald Kerr said. "The sooner, the better, my lass."

"And if it snows?" she asked him mischievously.

"We'll clear the road for ye, lass," he promised her.

There was no point in arguing with him any longer, Maggie thought. Fingal Stewart was already her husband under the laws of Scotland. To put him off any longer was to put Brae Aisir in danger. She already suspected this was the man who could beat her fairly. He was neither afraid of her nor intimidated by her. But she would do her very best, and he would not find it easy to overcome her.

"December fifth," she said.

The laird's face was immediately wreathed in smiles. "Done!" he replied. "Ye heard her, David. She said December fifth."

"I heard her, Dugald," the priest responded.

"I agree," Lord Stewart said.

Maggie laughed aloud. "You always seem to agree with me, my lord. You would, it appears, be a most reasonable man. I hope it continues after we are fully wed."

"I cannot promise, madam, for you are not always a biddable woman," he said.

Maggie nodded. "That is indeed true, my lord," she agreed. "I am not always easy, but I am usually right." She smiled sweetly at him.

Now Lord Stewart laughed.

Dugald Kerr was pleased by what he saw. His granddaughter seemed to be accepting of this marriage of the king's will. It all boded well but for one small detail.

Maggie and Fingal were rarely alone, if ever. They needed more time together, but how was he to accomplish it? And then he knew, and the solution was simple. "Maggie, lass," he said to her, "take Fingal to my library, and show him yer accounts. She's a clever girl, my lord, as you'll see when ye look at her books. No one can manage the accounts like my granddaughter."

"Och, Grandsire, I doubt Lord Stewart is interested in numbers," Maggie responded, but she was smiling at her elder.

"Nay, nay, I am quite interested," Fingal Stewart assured her. He understood what the old laird was about. He and Maggie did need some time alone, and it was unlikely they would get it in the hall filled with Brae

Aisir's men-at-arms not yet gone to their barracks for the night. Ordering them out of the hall would but give rise to talk.

Maggie stood up. "Very well," she said. "Come, and I will show you how I work my magic with numbers."

They departed the hall, and she brought him to her grandsire's library. It wasn't a particularly large chamber, but it was cozy with a small hearth that was already alight, and a row of three tall arched windows on one wall. Surprisingly there was a wall of books, some leatherbound, others in manuscript form. There was a long table that obviously served as a desk facing the windows, and a high-backed chair behind it at one end. Upon the desk were several leather-bound ledgers. Maggie opened one.

"I keep an account of every expenditure made," she said. "This is the account book for the household expenses. We are, of course, like most border keeps, self-sufficient but for a few things. The servants are paid for the year at Michaelmas as are the men-at-arms. The other books are records of the livestock bought and sold, the breeding book, and the book of the Aisir nam Breug," Maggie explained. "Since the beginning, a careful record has been kept of all those going south into England,

and coming north into Scotland. The Netherdale Kerrs keep a similar record."

"And ye do this yourself?" he asked.

"Aye. Grandsire says 'tis best we handle our own business," Maggie told him.

"How do ye fix the rate of the toll charge? Or is it simply a set rate?" he asked.

" 'Tis one rate for a single traveler or a couple, male and female. A merchant with a pack train of animals pays according to the number of animals he has. A peddler riding with everything on his back pays a set rate. There are fixed rates for wedding parties, families traveling together, messengers," Maggie explained.

" 'Tis well thought out," Lord Stewart remarked. "You note travelers in both directions though you collect tolls only one way," he noted. "Why?"

"To keep use of the traverse honest," Maggie said. "Over the centuries there have been times when some sought use of the Aisir nam Breug for less than peaceful purposes. We have caught the few and ejected them. Once we blocked the way. The watchtowers above the pass know who is in each party. We allow travel north from dawn in the morning, and south from the noon hour until sunset. In the dark months, travel alternates days going north Monday,

131

Wednesday, and Friday; and south Tuesdays, Thursdays, and Saturdays. Sundays the pass is closed but for emergencies such as a messenger."

"How long have the Kerrs on both sides of the border held this responsibility?" Lord Stewart asked.

"For more than five hundred years," Maggie told him.

How sad, Lord Stewart thought, that Maggie should be the last of the Kerrs of Brae Aisir. Perhaps he should add the Kerr name to his own. Others had done it in similar situations. Yet he was proud of his name. He would think on it.

"That is all I have to show ye," Maggie said, breaking into his thoughts. "Do ye have any questions to ask of me, my lord? If not, I should like to go to my chamber and bathe. We have another day of hunting ahead of us on the morrow."

"Stay," he said to her. "Can we not talk together?"

Maggie looked puzzled. "Talk? About what? Have ye questions?"

"Aye, questions about the girl who is my wife, yet not my wife," Fingal Stewart answered her. "Sit by the fire with me."

"There is only one chair," Maggie told him.

"Then sit in my lap," he said. "Or I can sit in yers," he teased.

She eyed him warily. "Sit in yer lap? Can I not answer yer questions standing? And what can ye possibly want to know about me? Why should it matter, for yer wed to me by the king's command, my lord."

"Aye, I am," he agreed pleasantly, "but what I know of ye so far, Maggie Kerr, I like. I would know more. And I would have ye like me."

"It doesn't matter," Maggie said bleakly. "We're wed."

"I was told ye had no other ye preferred," Lord Stewart said. "Have I taken ye from another who has engaged yer heart?"

"Nay, I don't," Maggie answered, "but I have never liked being told what I must or must not do, my lord. 'Tis childish, I know. Even if I might control the Aisir nam Breug alone, I canna bear an heir for Brae Aisir without a husband. Had there been a man among our neighbors who pleased me, I might have taken him as such, and shared the responsibilities of the traverse with him. But there was none. The young men fear me, for I am not a maid willing to sit by the hearth, and murmur yes, my lord, to a husband I canna respect, or one who does not respect me. I have said it often enough.

None of them wanted me for myself, but only for my wealth and power. So I chose none among them. They thought my grandfather was so desperate for a husband for me he would do whatever he had to do. But my grandsire knows me well, and he loves me. He understands my needs. But now King James has interfered in this matter." She sighed. "I will not let you win, Fingal Stewart. Ye must overcome me fairly."

"I will," he promised her.

"I know some think me selfish that I would have my way. I am not. I have controlled the Aisir nam Breug for almost three years now by myself. Grandsire is not well enough to do what must be done. I need a man who is willing to learn from a woman. That fool Ewan Hay was hardly the man."

"I have heard you beat him badly," Fingal Stewart remarked.

"I did!" Maggie admitted, restraining a wicked grin that threatened to break out upon her face. "I had to so he would give up and go away. I never expected the wretched weasel to go crying to the king. The damned fool had not a chance of outrunning me. Even if I had loved him, and I certainly did not, I could not have thrown the race, for everyone in the Borders knows there is none who can run as fast as

I do. I outran him and rode the course a-horse as he sat nursing his bloodied feet, the fool!"

"Yer a hard lass," Fingal Stewart said, his tone grudgingly admiring, "but to carry all the responsibility ye have carried, ye must be hard. But I can beat ye, Maggie Kerr, and I will." He sat down in the chair by the fire, and surprising her, reached out and yanked her into his lap. "That's better," he said. "Now tell me more about yerself, and I will tell ye about myself. I'd like us to at least be friends before I bed ye."

Maggie made a quick attempt to bolt, but Fingal Stewart pulled her back, his arm tightening about her.

"Nah, nah, lassie, yer my wife. A husband has the right to cuddle with his woman." His gray eyes caught her hazel eyes. "Have ye not cuddled with a sweetheart?"

"I've never had a sweetheart, my lord. Do ye think me wanton? I have more important things to be about," Maggie told him angrily. She was not comfortable. She didn't like being imprisoned by his arm. Her head had no place to go but his shoulder. She could smell the damp leather of his garments. It was strong, and it was too masculine. He reeked of power, and it frightened her. "Let me go," she said, attempting to keep her voice level and without fear. "Please release me, my lord."

"Yer afraid," he said, surprised. "Why are ye afraid?"

"I don't wish to be constrained," Maggie answered him.

He was silent a moment and then said, "I am but attempting to know my wife, lady. If I loosen my arm, will you remain in my lap for the interim? I know your word will be good."

"Ohh, that is so unfair!" Maggie cried softly.

"Why?" His tone was innocent of any deception, but they both knew better.

She laughed. She couldn't help it. "So you either hold me within yer embrace, or trust me to remain within it by my own choice," Maggie said. "And ye do not think it an unfair preference ye put before me?"

"Nay," he replied in the same bland tone. "Ye are too used to gaining yer own way, Margaret Jean Kerr. Now there will be times in the future when it will amuse me to let ye run headstrong as yer grandfather has done these seventeen years, but ye will not always have yer way with me. I'll be wearing the breeks in this family."

She stiffened. First with the use of her full Christian name — how had he known it? —

and then with her outrage at his speech. "Ohh, yer an arrogant man!" she told him. She was actually more at a loss for words than she had ever been. Never had she been spoken to in such a manner. She was Maggie Kerr, the heiress to Brae Aisir, damn it!

"Excellent!" he praised her. "Yer beginning to understand me. I am Fingal David Stewart, Lord of Torra and one day laird of Brae Aisir. I am arrogant, but not without cause. I descend from kings, lass, and the master of Scotland himself has sent me to marry ye, get bairns on ye, and keep the Aisir nam Breug as it has always been. My family has ever been faithful, and I will not shame them or their memory. Now will ye let me court ye, or will this be a war between us?"

His arm had loosened from about her. Maggie jumped from his lap. She had made him no promises, and she would make him none. "I don't know," she said in answer to his question. Then she ran from the library.

Fin sat before the small chamber's little hearth for some time after she had gone.

He had had enough experience with women to know she was confused and frightened. *God deliver me from skittish virgins,* Fingal Stewart thought to himself, but he knew that her fear of intimacy between them wasn't really the problem. Once he could kiss and caress her, he would win her over, and their bedsport would be pleasant, not that that mattered. Her duty would be to produce bairns for Brae Aisir; sons and daughters to ally them with other border families. But that wasn't the true difficulty between them.

It was control of the Aisir nam Breug that stood between them. The old laird had been wrong not to impress upon his heiress that it would be her husband controlling the pass, and not Mad Maggie Kerr. Still he had a great deal to learn about that traverse, and it was Maggie who would have to teach him for her grandfather was old. He had already turned his duties over to the lass. Oh, Fingal Stewart could beat his bride in the physical challenge she demanded. Of that he had no doubt, though others had failed. But it was his education regarding the Aisir nam Breug that would win Maggie's heart once she realized he could manage the responsibilities involved.

Martinmas came, and they still had not enough meat to last the winter. They hunted each day from dawn to dusk as the days shortened. Slowly the cold larder began to fill up. The meat from the deer they took was butchered. It hung alongside strings of rabbits, geese, and ducks. The boar, however, continued to elude them, but Maggie didn't care now that she was satisfied the keep and village were safe from starvation.

Like many border keeps, the Kerrs had royal permission to fish in the streams, rivers, and lochs in their area. They smoked and salted their catch, storing them in barrels. Dugald Kerr was a kindly man. He allowed the head of each household in his village to trap two coneys a month for their families and to lay away a small keg of salted fish. It was considered a generous gesture, especially given that the laird allowed them to grind in his mill the little grain they grew each growing season. The miller, of course, was allowed to take a tenth share for his trouble.

On St. Andrew's Day, Maggie pronounced the larder was filled to capacity. The weather was growing colder each day, and the nights were much longer now than they had been in September. The moat beneath the drawbridge was covered by a thin sheet of ice most mornings. It melted away during the daylight hours, but re-formed each night. Eventually it would not melt until spring. The stone walls of the keep began to show rimes of frost except in the few chambers where the hearths blazed. The men-at-arms began to sleep in the hall most nights now, for their barracks just within the walls had no hearth. In the stables and barn, those caring for the beasts slept with them in the hay for warmth.

The first day of December dawned sunny and unnaturally mild. A peddler asked shelter for the night. He would be traveling through the Aisir nam Breug in the morning. He had come from Perth via Stirling and Edinburgh. The peddler brought with him a large fund of gossip he was only too willing to share with the hall. He was surprised to learn the heiress to Brae Aisir had a husband, and one who had been sent by the king himself.

"Our Jamie has gone to France to seek a bride," he began, and he chuckled. "He's well funded to go courting, thanks to the church."

"What has the church to do with it?" the old laird asked.

"Why, sir, with these Protestant heretics rising up all over across the water, and even in England, our king's allegiance to Holy Mother Church is a valuable commodity for the pope to have. The king needs an income, and the church is wealthy. I heard he is to have seventy-two thousand Scots pounds over the next few years. 'Tis a fortune! And three of our most important abbeys and three priories of great consequence are to be given to his bastards for their income. He has six, and I'm told his latest mistress, Janet Munro, is with child." The peddler chortled. "Why, this fifth Jamie is every bit the man his da was, God bless him!" The peddler raised his tankard, drank to the king's health, and continued on with his gossip.

"They say he can have his choice of a wife from among the noble and royal families in Italy, France, and Denmark. That devil who rules England, King Henry, has even suggested a match with Princess Mary, his daughter," the peddler said. "And our Jamie has been presented with many diplomatic honors by those wooing him."

"The king prefers a French match," Lord Stewart said quietly.

"Aye! Aye! So he does," the peddler agreed. "They say the Duke of Vendôme is offering one hundred thousand gold crowns as a dower for his daughter, Marie. But the king turned the lass down."

"How on earth could you know that?" Lord Stewart demanded.

"Ah, sir, I passed through Leith recently. Word had just come that the king visited the court of the Duke of Vendôme in disguise. Despite her great dower, 'tis said he found the lady deformed and crippled. He left the duke's household quickly without making an offer for the lass. He has, it is said, fallen in love with Princess Madeleine, King François's daughter. It is reported she is a bonnie lass. The king offered for her, and the betrothal has been made. The marriage will be celebrated in January at the great Cathedral of Our Lady in Paris. We'll have a new French queen when the king brings her home," the peddler said, pleased to have been able to deliver this news to Brae Aisir.

But he had also gained some excellent gossip to pass on to the Netherdale Kerrs. It would gain him a night's lodging and a few meals in their hall on the morrow when he had traveled through the Aisir nam Breug. While he had told his tale standing before the high board, he had not, of course, been invited to be seated there. He was, after all, only a humble peddler. He had sat below the board with a trestle full of men-at-arms. It was there he had learned that the heiress to Brae Aisir's bridegroom was a cousin of King Jamie himself and had been sent by the king to wed Mad Maggie Kerr.

The contracts, he was told, had been signed weeks ago, but the couple had not yet bedded because Lord Stewart had yet to fulfill the famous challenge issued by the bride that was known throughout the Borders. The challenge was to take place on December fifth. The peddler wished he had an excuse to remain at Brae Aisir so he might relate firsthand what transpired. Looking at Fingal Stewart, however, he already knew. The man stood at least eight inches taller than the lass. He was muscled and in prime condition. If he couldn't outrun, outride, and outfight Mad Maggie Kerr, he didn't deserve to bed her.

The next day, however, dawned cold and rainy. The old laird invited the peddler to remain until the weather cleared. He accepted. He was in no hurry for he was on his way home to Carlisle where he would spend the winter months with his wife making another bairn. The peddler had plans. One day he intended to open a shop in the town, and it would be his sons he sent out to spend the spring, summer, and autumn months on the road while he remained behind in his shop. Word that he was in the keep had spread to the village. The women came to purchase ribbons, threads, needles, pins, and the fine lace trim he was known to carry. It turned into a profitable day, and when the peddler departed the following morning, he was in an excellent mood. The day might be cold, and the north wind had begun blowing, but he had a plump purse, and his wife was waiting for him at the end of his journey.

It took him the daylight hours to ride through the pass, leading his pack horses behind him. But as a weak sun was setting, he came in sight of Netherdale Hall where he was warmly welcomed by Lord Edmund. "Let me eat first, my lord, and then I shall bring you all the news I have gathered along my way," the peddler said. "I have some that will be of particular interest to you."

"Eat," Lord Edmund Kerr said, curious, but hardly anxious. The peddler was an unimportant fellow, but amusing, and the quality of his merchandise was excellent. "News of King James, I expect," he said.

"Aye, and of the Kerrs of Brae Aisir," the peddler replied as he dug a spoon into the wooden trencher of hot rabbit stew.

Lord Edmund raised an eyebrow but remained silent. To appear eager would make him look foolish. He would wait for the fellow to eat his meal. An imperceptible nod of his head brought a servant to fill his goblet. He sipped it slowly, thoughtfully, as he waited to learn the latest news. Had his cousin Dugald died? He doubted it. The old man for all his frailty was going to outlive them all.

Edmund Kerr had lived a half century. He had buried two wives. The first had given him six sons and three daughters. The second had borne three sons before she died in childbed with a sickly daughter. He was a handsome man with nut-brown hair just now being sprinkled with flecks of silver. He had the hazel eyes so many of the Kerrs on both sides of the border had. He stood six feet in height and was stocky with his age. And while he had a very satisfactory mistress, he wanted another wife.

Dugald Kerr would have to wed his granddaughter sooner than later. And who better to husband the wench than Edmund Kerr? He might even get a son or two on her, for a woman without children was prone to mischief. He had fathered several bastards. His mistress, Aldis, had given him a fine little daughter just a few months back. With nine legitimate sons to his credit, a new female child was more than welcome.

As for Maggie Kerr, his niece, he had seen her several times. She was a beauty, and his cock tightened in his breeks just thinking about her. A strong lass, she would make a fine wife for a man entering his old age — a young wife just like the king's, he thought.

But more important was that she was the heiress to Brae Aisir. That he was her uncle and that the Church might object meant nothing to him. She was only his half sister's child. He would have the lass no matter. When he wed her, the Aisir nam Breug would belong to him. He would use this new power to his own advantage.

The peddler finished his meal and, rising, went to stand before Lord Kerr's high board. He recounted all the gossip about King James while all in Netherdale Hall listened. Then clearing his throat, he delivered the newest tidbit in his arsenal. "The heiress to Brae Aisir has a husband," he said.

Edmund Kerr grew pale and then flushed with anger. "Say on, peddler," he commanded the man in a hard, tight voice.

"One of the lass's rejected suitors went to the king, complaining. 'Tis thought he believed King Jamie would order his marriage to Mad Maggie to protect the Aisir nam Breug. Instead, the king sent his cousin, Lord Fingal Stewart, instructing him to wed the lass, and take charge of the pass himself. Though he has not bedded her yet, the contracts making them man and wife were signed weeks ago," the peddler concluded.

"How do ye know he hasn't bedded her?"

Lord Edmund asked.

"The old laird has insisted Lord Stewart meet the conditions his granddaughter has set out. He must face her challenge to outrun, outride, and outfight her," the peddler explained to his host. "He'll win too, I expect. He's a big man with long legs."

Lord Edmund cursed softly beneath his breath. Why couldn't his life be simple? Now he would have to kill Lord Stewart, and widow the heiress. She could have no love for this stranger sent by her king. The death of an unwanted husband wouldn't matter to her at all. But it was hardly an auspicious way to begin a courting. "When will this challenge take place?" he asked the peddler. "Do ye know?"

"Oh, aye, my lord, I do. 'Twill be in three days time on the fifth of the month," answered the peddler. "I only wish I could be there to see it, but the weather is closing in, and I want to get home to Carlisle," the peddler said. "My wife and bairns are waiting."

Lord Edmund smiled and nodded with apparent understanding of the peddler's desires. "Of course," he murmured. "Travel with St. Christopher's blessing come the morrow. The news you brought has been most interesting and entertaining." Then the master of Netherdale Hall departed for his privy chamber.

His eldest son, who had been in the hall, heard the peddler's tale too. He knew his sire had planned on attempting to convince old Dugald Kerr to give him his heiress as his third wife. Unlike his father, however, Rafe Kerr was more of a realist. He doubted that the old laird would have so easily complied with his English relation's demand, and there was no love lost between the two family patriarchs. He almost laughed aloud at the thought of his father attempting to tame Maggie, his cousin.

Rafe had met up with her out on the moors several times and knew her for a hard woman. But Lord Edmund Kerr wasn't used to hard women. He liked meek, compliant wives, although one could hardly call his mistress, Aldis, meek. She was a hot-tempered bitch who usually managed to get her way with his father. And the old man positively doted on the wee bairn Aldis had birthed recently. She had done it, of course, so she might dig her claws deeper into Edmund Kerr, and while he might not realize it, she had succeeded. But while he didn't like Aldis, she kept his father occupied and away from trouble. But recognizing his father's ire, Rafe followed him into his privy chamber.

The older man whirled about. "What the hell do you want?" he snarled.

"What are you going to do?" Rafe asked. He was a younger, slender version of his sire. "If James Stewart is interested enough in the Aisir nam Breug to have sent blood kin to wed my cousin, then that's an end to it."

"Accidents happen," Edmund Kerr said ominously.

"Don't be a fool," Rafe said. "As long as the Scots kings knew little or nothing of the passage, you had the chance to take it all for us. That opportunity is gone now."

"James Stewart is interested in only one thing," Edmund Kerr said. "What he can gain from the Aisir nam Breug. I'm sure I can make the same arrangement with him that he has made with his cousin."

"You will cost us everything with your greed," Rafe said bluntly to his father.

Edmund Kerr went to strike his eldest a blow, but Rafe blocked him, his own thick fingers tightening about his father's wrist. His elder grew bright red in the face, his eyes almost popping from his head. Then he said, "Give over, my son, and hear me out."

Rafe loosened his grip, releasing his sire's

hand. "Nay, you hear me out, Da. But a third of the passage is in England. There is no argument or doubt about it. Yet our kinsmen in Scotland have shared the largesse of this traverse equally with us for centuries. If you succeeded in taking it all for yourself, you would be at the mercy of King Henry, who could force the use of the Aisir nam Breug for ulterior purposes. Then the Scots would retaliate, for the Kerrs' neighbors would certainly complain to their king. And then our most comfortable living would be gone, Da. It isn't worth it. My cousin has been wed by royal command. There's an end to it."

"But not bedded yet, which means there is no new heir in her belly," Edmund Kerr said. "If her husband were to die before he planted his seed, then she would need a new husband. There is nothing wrong with my taking her for my own wife if she is widowed. And I would have our son manage their part of the road when he was old enough. Nothing wrong with a father guiding his son, Rafe, is there? I guided and taught you."

"If you think the Scots king, now knowing of the Aisir nam Breug and its value, will let you marry my cousin and then take over the pass until a son you give her is grown, you have lost your wits, Da. And what if the bairn died? Maggie Kerr is like no woman you have ever met. You don't know her. All you can remember is a pretty lass you've seen now and again over the years. But I've seen her grown, Da. They don't call her *Mad Maggie* because she's a sweet young flower. She really can outrun, outride, and outfight any man in the Borders. And she's proud of it. Who the hell wants a termagant like that for a wife? And there is that little matter of consanguinity to consider."

"A couple of good beatings would cure her temper," Lord Edmund said.

"You wouldn't survive the first blow you aimed at her," Rafe said candidly. "She's a proud woman, Da." He noted his father's avoidance of the consanguinity.

"You sound as if you admire her," his father remarked.

"I do," Rafe replied. "I wouldn't want her in my bed, or birthing my bairns, and I especially would not want my daughters to be as independent as she is, but aye, I do admire her. I don't quite understand why I do. I think perhaps 'tis because she is like some magnificent wild creature, a falcon, an eagle, that cannot be tamed."

His father looked at him. "You're a damned romantic fool like your mother was," he said coldly. "However, you do not put me off the lass. Everything you have said intrigues me. With a woman like that by my side, we could make our own terms with both England and Scotland. We don't have to belong to either."

"What do you think Aldis will say to what you're considering?" Rafe asked wickedly. "She is hardly apt to stand by while you court and wed another. She'd kill you first. She gave you a bairn so she might bind you to her more closely."

"Wee Susan's a bastard just like a dozen or more others I've sired on various women hereabouts," Lord Edmund said. "Aldis is no fool. She knows her place."

Rafe Kerr laughed harshly. "Nay, Da, 'tis you who are the fool if you actually believe that. Aldis would be your wife. Marry her. She's a young wife for your old age."

"I want to go to Brae Aisir tomorrow," Lord Edmund Kerr said. "And I want you with me, Rafe. Let us meet this kinsman of Jamie Stewart, and see his mettle. And I want to be a spectator to this challenge between him and old Dugald's wench."

"That I will enjoy seeing myself," Rafe said enthusiastically. "The last man who attempted to win her was beaten so badly he has yet to raise his head from his shame, or so 'tis said. He was a Hay, I am told."

"We'll start out at first light," Lord Edmund said. "We should reach Brae Aisir by late afternoon. I doubt old Dugald will be glad to see me, but hearing of the wedding from our peddler friend, I could not resist coming to add my good wishes as the lord of the Netherdale Kerrs; especially as our two families will be working together to ensure the Aisir nam Breug remains the safe and peaceful route through the Cheviots it has always been." He smiled toothily at his oldest son, and Rafe laughed.

"You're a clever old devil, Da," he said. "Very well, let us go and size up the enemy. But I will wager you'll never get control of the whole road."

"We'll see," Lord Edmund Kerr replied to his eldest. "First things first, however, Rafe. Now I must go and have Aldis make certain I show at my best."

Rafe laughed all the harder. His father would have his mistress dress him in his best finery so he might go and court another man's wife. Aldis would hardly be pleased. Edmund Kerr was certainly a brave fellow, his son thought, amused. Brave or foolish, perhaps a bit of both; Rafe Kerr wasn't entirely sure which.

CHAPTER 5

The day dawned dry and cold. A weak sun hung low in the winter gray sky. Late the previous afternoon Brae Aisir had unexpected guests when Edmund Kerr and his son, Rafe, arrived. The sun had already set. Maggie welcomed them graciously, although she was suspicious of this sudden visit from their English kin. The old laird was less tactful than his granddaughter. Seated at the high board he glared down the hall as the visitors were announced and entered. His mouth was flint-thin with his disapproval of his English kin's arrival. His brown eyes grew hard with mistrust.

"Good evening, Cousin Dugald," Edmund Kerr said by way of greeting, though they were related in several ways. He bowed along with his son, smiling.

He wants something, Maggie thought. The smile showed too many teeth. She had never liked Edmund Kerr on the few occasions they had met when she was a child. This uncle reminded her of a fox, always looking at her as if she were something to eat, and he was just waiting for her to ripen and fall into his mouth.

"This is unexpected," Dugald Kerr replied to his kinsman's greeting. "What the hell brings ye to Brae Aisir on a winter's night, Edmund?"

"Bad news, Dugald," the Lord of Netherdale replied. "Bad news. I hosted a peddler a few nights past who said your heiress was wed by royal command. I cannot believe such a thing is true. Certainly you knew I would be offering for Margaret now that I have been widowed once again. With no male heir to follow you, a match between us is the perfect solution to keeping the Aisir nam Breug in the hands of the Kerr family. You would let strangers have our heritage, Dugald?"

The laird of Brae Aisir stood up, glaring down at his kinsman as he leaned over the high board, his broad hands flat upon its smooth surface. "Brae Aisir is Scotland, Edmund, not England. I was glad to give Maggie into the keeping of a good Scots husband, the king's kinsman, I might add. Besides, ye don't need a wife. Ye've had two. Ye've a quiver full of bairns. Ye've a mistress the gossips say is jealous of any female who casts an eye upon ye. There's even a rumor she helped yer last wife to her death. Yer Maggie's uncle, for God's sake! She is wed to Fingal Stewart, and that's an end to it. I'll give ye and yer lad shelter tonight, but on the morrow I expect ye both gone back through the Aisir nam Breug. I dinna hope to see ye again." Dugald Kerr sat back down.

"The marriage hasn't been consummated," Edmund Kerr said boldly. "It could be annulled by the archbishop in York."

The laird leaned back in his chair. "Yer balls are as wizened as yer brain, Edmund," he said. "Yer too close in blood for me to have ever considered such a match. For sweet Jesu's sake, her mam was yer half sister. The marriage will be blessed tomorrow by the keep's priest, and consummated soon after. Why the hell would I turn away King James's own kinsman, a strong vital Scot, for an ancient Englishman?"

A snicker rippled through the hall from the men at the trestles.

"I'm young enough to have just sired another child," Edmund Kerr said angrily.

"I'm sure ye labored mightily to get that bairn, if indeed it's yers," the laird replied.

Now there was open laughter among the

men-at-arms.

"My father is disappointed, as would any man be to lose such a lovely young woman as the lady Margaret," Rafe Kerr said in an attempt to ease the situation. His father was looking more foolish with each word he uttered.

"Are ye the eldest?" Dugald Kerr asked the young man.

"Aye, my lord," Rafe responded.

"The heir?"

"Aye, my lord. I am Rafe Kerr."

"Ye look to have more sense than yer sire, laddie. This is Fingal Stewart, Maggie's husband," he said, indicating with a wave of his hand Lord Stewart, who sat on his right. "Ye two will be doing business together eventually. Ye should get to know each other. Busby! A goblet of wine for young Rafe Kerr, and his sire too. Come up and join us at the high board, laddie." He looked to Edmund. "Sit down, Edmund. I don't like ye, and never have, but yer heir looks to have promise."

"Go on," Edmund Kerr hissed at his son, and then he seated himself on a bench at the nearest trestle, taking the goblet offered and drinking deeply.

The younger man joined those at the high board, seating himself next to Lord Stewart. The two men began talking.

The old laird chuckled.

"I almost feel sorry for Lord Edmund," Maggie said to the laird. "Ye were very hard on him, Grandsire."

"Pompous fool," Dugald Kerr muttered. "And the nerve of him to think I would ever consider giving my darling lass to him to wife."

"He doesn't want me, Grandsire. He wants to control the entire Aisir nam Breug," Maggie replied. "You know that's why he has hotfooted through the traverse this day."

"Even if ye were a perfect match for him, I wouldn't have allowed it," Dugald Kerr said. "This is Scotland. We may be in the Borders, but the boundary between Scotland and England has always been clear in the pass. Ye needed a Scots husband, and ye have one now."

"Only if he beats me on the morrow," Maggie said.

The laird nodded. "He will," he said with surety.

Maggie laughed. "Have ye lost faith in me then, Grandsire?"

"I'll never lose faith in ye, lass, but this man is the man for ye."

Maggie was not about to agree with her

grandfather. At least not yet. But she had to admit that the past few weeks had been a revelation to her. They had hunted together, and he had not treated her like some delicate creature. He had treated her like an equal. But once the marriage was blessed and consummated, would he behave the same way? He was learning the business of the Aisir nam Breug from her quickly. Her grandfather noted it and was pleased.

She and Fingal had visited every one of the watchtowers along the miles under Scots control. He spoke with the men, and the men liked him. He saw where repairs were needed for both the towers and the narrow stone road. He had asked her who originally built the road, and she had told him no one was really certain, but it was probably a people known as the Romans who had built the wall that was the divide between England and Scotland. He wanted to know how the Aisir nam Breug became the Kerr family's responsibility.

Maggie had explained that the family traced its roots to an Anglo-Norman family who sent several of their number north in the eleventh century. Two brothers had discovered the stone road deep within the hills. They had divided it, the elder taking the larger section and settling in Scotland,

and the younger taking the small section and settling in England. Lord Stewart had nodded. Those were the days when a man could go forth and make his own fortune, and found a dynasty.

Seeing her grandfather, her husband, and Rafe Kerr deep in conversation, she slipped from the table to seek out Busby. "See two bedspaces nearest one of the hearths are made ready for Lord Edmund and his son," she instructed the servant. "And send Clennon Kerr and Iver Leslie to me in the library."

"Aye, m'lady. Is there anything else I can do for ye this evening?" Busby inquired solicitously. "I know the race will be run on the morrow."

"Make sure the breakfast served afterwards is hearty," Maggie said with a twinkle in her hazel eyes. "I imagine his lordship will be quite worn-out attempting to win the challenge."

Busby chuckled. "Aye, my lady," he said. "I'll tell Cook to make it a festive meal for ye." Then he asked with the familiarity of a man who had known her since her birth, "Do ye think he can beat ye, my lady?"

"Perhaps," Maggie said slowly. "Dinna say I said it, Busby, but the man has long legs."

Then with a grin she hurried off to the library.

Clennon Kerr and Iver Leslie quickly joined her.

"I want a hearth built in the barracks," Maggie told them. The hall isn't large enough to comfortably hold all the men at night, but the barracks are too cold now that winter is about to descend upon us. Before the weather becomes bad, the hearth and its chimney must be built. The hunt is over. The cattle and sheep are in the home meadows. The men have more than enough time on their hands. Have them gather all the materials they will need before they open the wall up. And be certain they cover the opening at night so the weather doesn't get into the barracks."

"Yes, m'lady," Clennon Kerr said. "Is there anything else?"

"Nay, and I'm off for bed. I need my rest before tomorrow's race," Maggie said.

Iver Leslie grinned. "He's fast, m'lady," he told her.

"God's toenail, I hope so," Maggie answered him. "My last suitor ran like a lass." And then she left the two men who were guffawing loudly at her remark. She had told Grizel no bath this evening, but she would surely need one after tomorrow's race. She had sent Grizel to her own bed; Maggie had no need of her, being perfectly able to wash and undress herself.

Tomorrow, she thought as she finally lay abed. Fingal Stewart was the first man she had ever considered having the ability to beat her in fair combat. She had been running the hills about Brae Aisir for so long, she couldn't remember when she had first begun. Her grandsire said she was just past two when she had disappeared over the drawbridge one day, giving them all a terrible fright until she came running back up the path from the village. It was quickly observed that Maggie Kerr could run very fast. By the time she was four, the village lads were running with her, and by the time she was six, it was acknowledged that no one could run as fast as she could run.

Tomorrow, however, her reign as the fastest person in the Borders could easily come to an end. And if it did, then she would have to accept Fingal Stewart as her husband. She had to admit to herself that he had been very patient with her waiting to consummate the marriage. She had put all thoughts of consummation from her mind these past weeks ever since the marriage contracts had been signed, making her legally his wife. She felt a bit guilty about that day, for she had not dressed herself in a beautiful gown for the signing. She had the Aisir nam Breug to show him, and signing the documents that would make them man and wife was but a bit of legal business to be swiftly concluded. She had dressed as she usually did, but then so had he.

And on the morrow they would both be dressed for their combat. But afterwards, she promised herself, she would dress herself properly for the blessing of their union, and the feast to come. Mad Maggie Kerr might be considered a hoyden by most who knew her, but she did know how to dress like a lady. There was that wonderful burgundy velvet gown trimmed in marten in her wardrobe she might wear, or perhaps the dark green velvet with the gold trim. To her surprise, she fell asleep considering her gowns, but she had awakened before dawn, her head clear. Climbing from her bed, she ran to the window to see what kind of a day it would be. It was gray, but on the horizon a weak sun was just struggling to rise. To her relief there seemed to be no wind as the bare trees stood black in stark relief against the light sky. The water in the moat was liquid, not ice. It hadn't frozen the past night, which meant it was warmer despite the month.

Without waiting for Grizel, Maggie opened the trunk at the foot of her bed and pulled out a pair of breeks. They were soft with age, and she always wore them when she ran. Yanking off her night shift, she dressed herself quickly. First came a cotton chemise that just reached her midthighs. Then came her shirt and breeks with a leather belt to hold them up. She ran a brush through her hair, then tied her rich brown locks back with a scarlet ribbon. "I'm ready!" she said aloud as Grizel entered her bedchamber.

"Yer eager then," her tiring woman said. "Well, so is everyone else. The laird is in the hall with Father David and the Netherdale Kerrs. I passed yer husband on the staircase coming down as I was coming up for ye."

"Then 'tis time," Maggie agreed.

"I'll bring yer boots and stockings for the riding," Grizel said, picking up the items as she spoke. Then she quickly followed her mistress downstairs.

"Good morrow, all," Maggie greeted them, bounding into the hall.

"Good morrow," they greeted her back.

"Are ye ready, Granddaughter?" Dugald Kerr asked her solemnly.

"I am, my lord."

"And ye, Fingal Stewart, are ye ready?"

"I am, my lord."

"Then let us go out to the courtyard where the race will begin and end," the laird said as he led the way. Once outside, he spoke to them both. "This will be a harder challenge. A footrace across the drawbridge, down the path into the village, through the village, around the kirk at the end of the village, and back the same way. The second part of the challenge is a horse race that follows the same path as the footrace but for one exception. Before ye may recross the drawbridge, ye must ride about the keep once. The final part of the challenge is a combat with claymores to be held here in the courtyard.

"When first blood is drawn, the match is over. If either of you cannot finish any part of the challenge, your opponent is declared the winner. Do ye both understand the rules of this competition?"

"I do, my lord," Fingal Stewart said.

Maggie nodded. Then she looked at Lord Stewart and said in an almost defiant tone, "I run in bare feet, my lord."

Fingal smiled at her. "I don't," he said in a pleasant voice.

"Do ye not think that gives ye an advantage?" she demanded of him.

"Nay, I think 'tis ye who has the advantage, madam, but 'tis a cold morning. I prefer to keep my boots on," he answered. "But I'll be happy to wait to begin this contest between us if ye decide ye will wear yers."

"She's clever," Rafe Kerr said softly to his father.

"How so?" Lord Edmund wanted to know.

"She's used to the track she'll travel in her bare feet. In boots the road would not be familiar. She could stumble, and lose time. But her bare feet know the path very well." Rafe said. He shook his head admiringly. "She's a braw lass, Da."

"Are ye ready then?" the laird asked the two combatants, and when they nodded in the affirmative he said, "Then we begin. On yer marks. Get set. Go!"

Maggie leaped forward. The wood of the drawbridge felt firm and sure beneath her bare soles. Her feet knew the way well, and with each pump of her legs her speed increased. She breathed rhythmically, and knew she would not begin to feel even slightly winded until she was crossing the drawbridge again. Head high she ran, and before long she felt the ribbon holding her hair begin to loosen, and then it flew away. As her long hair blossomed about her, she heard the triumphant cry of the lass who had caught the ribbon. It was an unspoken rule that when Mad Maggie Kerr's ribbon blew off during a race, only a woman might have it. The single street of the village was lined with Kerr clansmen and women watching the lady meet her latest challenge.

She was about to turn her head to see how far behind her he was when a movement by her side caught her eye. Maggie swiveled her head slightly and to her astonishment found herself looking into the face of Fingal Stewart. And she realized he was running as easily as she was. He grinned wickedly at her. As they raced around the kirk at the end of the street, Maggie increased her speed; however, to her surprise, he kept up with her. As they raced back down the village street, she began to feel a burning in her lungs. She was racing, she realized, faster than she had ever raced before.

They were both breathing hard as they struggled up the path to the keep. Maggie forced a final burst of speed as she reached the drawbridge and pounded across it. But Fingal Stewart would not be beaten, meeting her speed with his own. Together they raced into the courtyard, shoulder to shoulder and gasping for air as they did.

" 'Tis a tie!" Dugald Kerr shouted. "Well done, Maggie and Fin! Well done!"

But Maggie wasn't listening to her grand-sire's praise. In a final sprint, she dashed across the courtyard barefoot, and leaped upon her stallion's back, urging the beast from the keep's enclosure. At first surprised that she would not take a moment to accept the congratulations of those assembled, Fin-gal Stewart followed her lead, exhorting his stallion to follow and catch up with her.

Maggie flattened herself as she leaned forward on the stallion's neck, goading him onward. No man had ever beaten her in a footrace. None had ever come close. Yet Fingal Stewart had tied her, and done it fairly. Worse, she suspected he could have even done it in his bare feet, though he chose to wear his boots. Had he worn them to give her the advantage? God's foot! Now she would always wonder, and she could hardly ask him because had he tried to give her the advantage, it would seem a paltry thing to do.

Then her ears caught the sound of hoof-beats as his stallion caught up with hers. The two beasts screamed at one another rearing up, teeth bared, their hooves strik-ing out as their riders sought to get them under control and racing again. It had been madness to pit two ungelded males against one another, but neither Maggie nor Fin was willing to ride another horse.

"I told ye this would happen," he shouted at her as the villagers scattered away from the half-battling stallions.

"Do ye want to admit defeat?" she taunted him as she yanked her horse's head around, and kicked it into a gallop again.

His laughter was her answer. They raced down the village street, around the kirk, and back towards the keep. He kept his animal just a pace behind her to avoid another battle between the two stallions. He fully intended pushing his horse ahead of hers as they reentered the courtyard. They reached the top of the path again, and dashed about the stone keep. Maggie was certain the victory would be hers, and when it was, it wouldn't matter who won the combat by sword. There would be no clear-cut winner, for to win this challenge, one combatant had to win all three contests. Her stallion clambered onto the drawbridge again, his hooves pounding against the wood of the bridge. But to Maggie's surprise, Fingal Stewart's stallion was suddenly once again head to head with hers as they galloped into the yard and came to a screeching halt.

" 'Tis a dead heat once more!" the old laird declared delightedly.

The two sweating stallions stood with wild

eyes, foam about their mouths, and heaving sides as their riders slid from their backs. They were too tired to renew the fight between them as the stable lads led them away to separate ends of the stables to recover.

"Will ye be battling me with yer claymore in yer bare feet?" Fingal Stewart asked her, grinning.

"Will ye take off yer boots too, or are yer dainty feet still too cold?" Maggie mocked him, returning the grin.

"Put yer socks and boots on, lassie," the laird told his granddaughter. "Ye should have done so before ye mounted that big beast of yers to race."

"It didn't affect my riding," Maggie said, seating herself upon the stone steps into the house. She pulled on the warm knit stockings Grizel handed her, and then her boots. Upon standing she said, "I'm ready now."

Clennon Kerr, the keep's dour captain, handed Maggie her claymore. It was a fine weapon, fifty-five inches in length with a cross handle. It was a plain sword with no fancy or decorative embellishments about it. The captain handed Fingal Stewart an identical weapon. "They're the same blade, my lord," he said.

"So I see," Lord Stewart answered. He

had quickly come to trust Clennon Kerr, for Iver liked him, which he would not have had the captain been duplicitous. And an almost imperceptible nod from Iver told him all was well.

A chair, brought from the hall, was set upon the top step leading to the hall. The laird settled himself into the chair, his English kinsmen standing by his side. He would be able to clearly see everything from his position. Below them the keep's men-at-arms formed a circle, and the two combatants stepped into it. They were garbed as they had come from the hall that morning, and wore no mail to protect them.

"Remember," Dugald Kerr said in a stern voice, "this contest between ye both ends when first blood is drawn. Try not to injure each other seriously. It is a battle of skill between ye. Naught else. I will stop it if either of ye displays undue roughness. Ye may now begin."

Their weapons required that they fight with two hands. Grasping the hilts of their claymores, they raised them in a salute to each other, and then metal met metal with a horrific clanging. Fingal Stewart was not surprised by Maggie's skill with her claymore. With any other woman he might have been, but he had found her to be a woman not given to bragging. If she said she was proficient in something, he accepted that she was, and she had said she could wield a claymore as well as any. She could. It took all his skill to keep from being blooded by her.

He didn't know why he cared other than the fact that a man, especially one who would one day control an important ingress into Scotland, should not be vanquished by a woman; yet he was uncomfortable with the reality that to win this contest between them he must blood her. If he could wear her down eventually perhaps she would yield to him without the necessity of it. But Maggie was a stubborn woman. Unless he won all three challenges, Fingal Stewart knew she would not respect him. Of course, the first two contests between them had ended in a tie, so if he had not beaten her, he had at least equaled her, which should gain him a modicum of her respect. But he knew that this last battle between them must yield a clear winner, and he had to be that winner.

He had spent the past few minutes keeping her at bay. Now he began to fight her in earnest, raising his claymore with two hands, the blade striking hers fiercely as she blocked his attack. The clash of the two blades reverberated through her entire body, and Maggie staggered, surprised. She suddenly found herself on the defensive against him, and she realized he meant to win here unequivocally where he had not won before. She stiffened her spine, and fought hard driving him back, back, back, step by step by step.

"Jesu, she fights like a man," Lord Edmund said, not realizing until his son laughed that he had spoken aloud.

"Still want her for a wife, kinsman?" the laird of Brae Aisir asked mockingly of his Netherdale cousin. "She's more woman than any ye have ever known."

"She's magnificent," Rafe said. "I hope we never meet in battle."

"Yer a wise man, laddie, unlike yer sire," Dugald Kerr told him.

"A lass belongs in the hall directing her servants," Edmund Kerr said, finally speaking. "Not in the yard in breeks fighting with a man. Ye've let her run wild, Dugald. I don't envy her husband. I hope he can successfully bed that wildcat of yours. He'll have to if yer to get a male heir."

"Tonight," the laird told him. "Look closely, Edmund. My Maggie is beginning to tire. Fingal Stewart is a strong opponent. And his patience is coming to an end."

"Aye," Rafe noted softly, "she's tiring. I'm sorry to see it, for she's a brave lass."

She was his wife, damn it! Fingal Stewart thought as he realized that Maggie was not going to give up. And he wanted her, not because a king had matched them to serve his own needs or even because it was his right, but because he was coming to love the stubborn wench. She was everything a man could want in a wife — noble, brave beyond measure, and loyal. She was honest to a fault, firm but kind to her servants, and the villagers would not have been so devoted to her had she not had all of these virtues. And with a modicum of total honesty he had to admit she was a beauty. Aye, Mad Maggie Kerr was everything a wife should be. *His wife.*

There she stood. Her capable hands gripped the hilt of her claymore as she fought him. Her shirt was wet beneath the arms, sticking to her back and breasts. She was gasping for breath, and near to falling on her face with her exhaustion, but she would not give up. The marriage was fact. The contest before the consummation had been to satisfy any discontent among the Kerrs' neighbors that the king's kinsman had had his bride dishonestly. His forbearance at an end, Fingal Stewart raised his claymore even as Maggie raised hers against him. With a mighty blow, he knocked the sword from her hand, over the heads of the men-at-arms encircling them, and across the courtyard.

Maggie fell to her knees, the force of the two weapons meeting having gone right through her. She knelt there in the dust, unable for a moment to arise, for her legs seemed unable to function at all. Everything ached — her shoulders and her arms, her neck, the palms of her hands. Her fingers were suddenly weak. She heard Grizel's cry of distress.

As she raised her head, her eyes suddenly filled with tears. She looked to her grandfather, ashamed to have failed, and Maggie knew she had indeed failed.

"My lord?" Fingal Stewart's calm voice queried. Then he said, "I know the rules ye have set for this contest, but I will not, cannot blood a woman in combat. We have both fought fairly, and the only blood I will take from Maggie Kerr is that which belongs to her maidenhead and is rightfully mine. If there is a winner to this swordplay, then ye must declare such, my lord." Then he bent, reaching out to draw Maggie to her feet, his strong arm going about her waist to hold her against his side. "Yer a braw lass," he said low so that only she could hear him, "but I'm not as young as ye are, and ye've fair worn me out, madam. Give over now, and let there be peace between us, Maggie mine."

Unable to help herself, Maggie nodded, giving him a weak, cheeky grin in reply.

"Enough!" Dugald Kerr responded in a surprisingly loud and strong voice. "I declare this challenge over. Both contestants have won in the footrace and the riding, but 'tis Fingal Stewart who has won the battle of the claymores. I name him the winner, and let none say otherwise." He looked straight at his granddaughter as he spoke. "Margaret Jean Kerr, will ye accept this man, Fingal Stewart, as yer true husband in every way a man is husband to his wife?"

"I will!" Maggie declared loudly so that all heard her. "He has even before this day gained my admiration, but today he has gained my respect. I will be his wife proudly and gladly in every way in which a woman is wife to her husband."

Fingal Stewart turned Maggie so she faced him, bending down to give her mouth a long and hot kiss as cheers erupted about them. He would have carried her off this moment had he not known more was expected of them that day than just a coupling.

Jesu! Her mouth was the sweetest he had ever known, and he couldn't stop kissing her.

Her head spun riotously with the kiss. She had known a stolen kiss on her cheek here and there to which she had always responded by smacking the bold lads, yet never but once before had she known a kiss like this one. Their lips locked together seemed to engender a ferocious heat. She slid her arms up about his neck, pressing herself against him with a need she didn't quite understand at all. Was it lust? Was it love?

He felt his cock swelling within his breeks. Jesu! She was going to love as fiercely as she had lived. The thought was intoxicating, and he held her even closer, wanting her to know his need. Pulling her head away from his, Maggie's surprised eyes met his. "I think they all know we have made our peace now, madam," he said to her in a level voice. "If we kiss any more, I fear yer grandsire will have to throw a bucket of cold water over us, Maggie mine."

"I've never known a man, for all that's said of me," she responded softly. "Ye'll be gentle, Fingal, my lord?"

" 'Tis December, Maggie mine, and the nights are long," he replied for her ears alone. "I'll be gentle, and we'll love at our leisure, for we have a lifetime ahead of us."

"I'll want to bathe and change my battling clothing for wedding finery before Father David blesses our union," Maggie told him.

"Then I shall do the same," he said as the circle of grinning men surrounding them broke open to allow them to pass through.

They walked up the stairs to where her grandfather still sat. Dugald Kerr was smiling broadly at them both. "Well done, both of ye," the old laird said. "I'm proud that my great-grandchildren will come from such strong stock. Make me a lad first."

"With yer permission, my lord, we will want to bathe and change into more suitable garments before the blessing," Fin said to Dugald Kerr.

The laird nodded. "Go along then," he said as with his consent they turned and left him. Dugald Kerr stood up now. He looked at his English kinsmen. "Go home," he told them. "There is nothing for you here at Brae Aisir."

"I'd prefer to remain until the morrow," Lord Edmund told his kinsman. "Surely ye will want yer relations at the blessing, the feast, and to attest to the honesty of the bride," he said in silky tones.

"Da!" Rafe was not pleased, for he realized his father had not yet given up on his impossible dream of uniting the two families and thereby putting the pass under the control of a single person, namely himself.

Dugald Kerr laughed harshly. "Jesu, Edmund, was being party to the challenge not enough for ye? Very well then, stay. But fair or wet, ye'll go on the morrow if I have to escort ye myself." Then turning, he stamped back into his warm hall.

"Are ye mad?" Rafe asked his parent. " 'Tis over and done with, Da. They'll bed tonight, and from the look of them both, Brae Aisir will have an heir in less than a year."

"Aye," his father said. "But a bairn is a fragile creature, Rafe. I've fathered enough of them and buried enough of them to know that."

Rafe Kerr looked hard at his father. "If I thought you would dare such a thing, Da, I'd kill you myself," he said.

Lord Edmund looked at his eldest son in surprise. "We could control the whole Aisir nam Breug. Why would you not want that? Our power in the Borders, both sides, would be enormous. We would collect the tolls going both ways. What do you find repugnant about that, Rafe?"

"Everything," his son replied. "Have you

no wisdom about this, Da? We borderers own but scant loyalty to our kings. We rule ourselves on both sides of the border. The traverse has been kept honest and free of strife because the *two* branches of our family have controlled it over the centuries. No king has told us what to do. We decided *together* long ago that the pass would be used only for peaceful travel. We set the tolls *together. Together* we built the watchtowers that oversee the route. We have stood *together* against any who would use the Aisir nam Breug for illicit purposes.

"Do we not have enough strife among our families here in the Borders, Da? One family on either side of the march controlling the pass would open it to all manner of evil. A king could interfere and claim the land for his own. They dare not do it with two families in control. Bribery would ensue, and not necessarily with the lord ruling the pass, but among the men guarding it who would look the other way if paid to do so. They would open the Aisir nam Breug to smugglers and raiders. But with the two families ruling the road, it is too difficult for such dishonesty to flourish. It might have been us, Da, whose direct line expired. Would you have wanted old Dugald Kerr to take your responsibilities away from your designated heir?"

"We could be richer than we are if we had the entire traverse," Lord Edmund said.

"I am your heir, Da, and I will not support you in this foolishness," Rafe said. "I like Lord Stewart, from what little I have learned of him in our conversations. When old Dugald dies or decides to give up his responsibility, Fingal Stewart will manage his end of the road well. He's an honorable man."

"You're a fool," his father replied. "How fortunate that I have other sons."

Rafe Kerr laughed. He was the most capable of all Edmund Kerr's sons, legitimate and born on the wrong side of the blanket. When they were all children, his father had made it a point to teach the younger of his siblings unquestioned loyalty and obedience to Rafe, for Rafe — as his father was constantly pointing out to the others — was the heir. And Rafe had enforced their sire's teachings as he had grown. Each of his brothers had his trust and loyalty in return. And if there was one thing of which he was entirely certain, it was that not one of them wanted all the responsibilities that went along with being the heir to Edmund Kerr, and overseeing their part of the Aisir nam Breug. "Give over, Da, and enjoy the day," he said. "The laird's wine cellars will be open wide today." Then putting an arm about his father's shoulders, he walked with him back into the hall.

Around them the servants were dashing about setting the high board. The trestles and the benches were brought from an alcove of the hall where they were stored when not in use. Barrels of October ale were rolled in. Small wheels of hard yellow cheese were placed on each trestle. A linen cloth edged in lace was laid over the high board. A large silver gilt saltcellar in the shape of the sun in its splendor, which was the Kerr family's crest, was set upon it. Silver goblets studded with green agate were placed at the six places being set with round silver plates, spoons, and forks. Each guest had his or her own knife.

"Old Dugald has forks," Lord Edmund noted. "Why don't we have forks in our hall?" he grumbled.

"Aldis suggested them, but you wouldn't pay the cost," Rafe reminded him. "You said the Florentine merchants were smiling thieves in silk clothing."

"Humph," Lord Edmund said. "Tell her she can get them. And I want a dozen. Dugald probably has a dozen. We can't be lacking."

A servant brought them wine, and they joined their host by the fire as they awaited the bride and bridegroom.

Maggie had hurried to her chamber to find her large tub set up, the serving men just bringing in the last buckets of hot water. When they had poured it into the oak tub, Grizel shooed them out. Then she pulled off Maggie's boots and socks. The girl stood, slipped her breeks down over her hips, and, kicking them away from her, unlaced her shirt, drawing it off, and finally her short chemise. Then without a moment's hesitation she stepped up the wood steps and down into the tub. "God's blood!" she swore softly. "I ache in every joint, Grizel. I must soak a moment or two before I wash."

"Ye fought hard," Grizel said proudly. "It was a grand contest and will be spoken of in the Borders for many years to come."

"Few saw it but our own," Maggie reminded her tiring woman.

"They'll repeat it to their kin who were not here today, and they will pass it on to others throughout the Borders," Grizel said.

"God only knows how the tale will end up, for it will be embellished by each person who repeats it," Maggie said, laughing softly.

"He's a fine man, and will give ye strong sons and daughters, mistress," Grizel said. "Is there anything ye would ask of me now that ye face yer wedding night?"

"Nay," Maggie replied, a faint blush touching her cheeks. "I've seen enough lasses and lads in the hay and out on the moors to know just enough to make a beginning of it. And what I don't know I expect that my husband will tutor me in to make up for my deficiencies."

"Aye," Grizel agreed. " 'Tis better that way, for ye'll learn to please him. And ye'll get yer way more often than not pleasing a husband than displeasing him."

"Help me wash my hair," Maggie said, changing the subject. "My scalp is soaked wet with all my efforts this morning."

Grizel brought her mistress a small stone jar filled with scraps of soap that had been melted soft in a bit of water. Taking a small pitcher, she dipped it into the tub and poured the water over her mistress's head. Then Maggie dipped her fingers into the jar, bringing up a handful of the mixture, which she rubbed into her head. The sweet-smelling mixture foamed up quickly as she scrubbed her head. Grizel rinsed the soap away, and the two women repeated the process. When all the soap was finally erased from Maggie's hair, she took her tresses into a hank, wringing it out. Then Grizel pinned the wet hair atop the girl's head so she might continue her bath.

"I can't decide whether to wear the burgundy or the deep green velvet," Maggie said to her companion as she scrubbed herself.

"Neither," Grizel surprised her by replying. "I've been working for weeks on a gown for ye to wear on this day, my lady." She chuckled, well pleased by the look of excitement that bloomed on Maggie's face. "Finish with yer bath," Grizel said, smiling.

"Do ye think my lord has bathed too?" Maggie wondered aloud.

"Aye, he has," Grizel answered her.

"How can ye know?" Maggie inquired.

"Archie is a man who enjoys a bit of chatter," Grizel said, chortling. "He said he was putting sandalwood oil in his master's bathwater today."

"My lord's manservant likes ye," Maggie teased her tiring woman.

"Do ye ache less now?" Grizel asked, avoiding the subject of Lord Stewart's man.

"Aye," Maggie replied, but her hazel eyes were twinkling. "I don't think I have ever in my life fought so hard as I did this day. My husband is very skilled with his claymore.

Not once did he give me the opportunity to slip beneath his guard and blood him," she said admiringly.

"Did ye want him to?" Grizel inquired slyly.

Maggie smiled almost to herself. "Nay," she admitted. "I didn't."

"He's a bold man, and an honorable one too," Grizel said, nodding approvingly.

Maggie finally emerged from her tub. The water was cooling, and she was beginning to ache again. She dried herself thoroughly, wrapping the cloth about herself. Then she sat down by her hearth to get warm again while she toweled her hair with another cloth and began brushing it out before the fire.

" 'Tis past noon," Grizel said at last. "Ye must dress, and then go to the kirk for the blessing. The Netherdale Kerrs haven't left. They're staying for the blessing and the feast. Lord Edmund is not happy about yer marriage, but Rafe, yer cousin, seems a good lad. Not at all like his da. Imagine the old fool telling yer grandsire that he wanted to wed ye and bring the two families together," Grizel said indignantly.

"He wants to control all of the Aisir nam Breug," Maggie said. "I seem to be the answer to his desire. I'd nae wed him if he were the last man on earth, and as fair as a May morn," Maggie said. "I've never liked him, even as a child."

Grizel took the hairbrush from her mistress, and running it through the girl's hair said, "Yer dry now. Let's get ye dressed, my lady."

Maggie could see her undergarments laid out upon her bed, but there was no sign of a gown. Grizel handed her mistress a pair of soft woolen stockings that were pale in color and came just below her knee. She drew them on, affixing them with a plain ribbon garter. Standing, she next put on a chemise. It had long sleeves trimmed with gold lace, and a low square neckline also edged in gold lace that would match her gown's neckline. Next Grizel added two silk petticoats that tied in the back with ribbon.

The tiring woman went to the wardrobe and drew out the bodice, which already had its sleeves affixed, and the skirt that made up the gown that Maggie would wear. The lower half of the gown was a funnel skirt of orange tawny velvet brocade edged in brown fur. The matching velvet bodice had a square neckline edged in gold embroidery, and the sleeves had deep turned-back cuffs of rich brown marten, the gold lace from her chemise sleeves just barely visible.

"Well?" Grizel said, smiling.

"It's beautiful!" Maggie exclaimed. "It's perfect!" She threw her arms about the older woman. "Thank you, Grizel! Thank you!"

"I want the king's kinsman to see what a fine lady ye are," Grizel said. "I want him to know yer the kind of wife he can take to court one day when the king takes a wife. I want him to be proud of ye as all here at Brae Aisir are proud of ye." She wiped a tear or two from her warm brown eyes.

Maggie was close to tears herself after Grizel's declaration. "Help me finish dressing," she said, a catch in her voice. What on earth was the matter with her today? She supposed it was the shock of actually losing the contest. Before this day no one seeking her hand who had dared to take up the challenge had ever gotten past the footrace, although she had raced her stallion just to make a point with Ewan Hay. The contracts had been signed weeks ago. She was already wed to Fingal Stewart. But now he had gained her respect. He had proved himself worthy to be her husband this day, to inherit control of the Aisir nam Breug eventually, to sire bairns upon her.

She stood silently as Grizel fastened the skirt of her gown. It fell in graceful folds over her petticoats. She slid her arms into the bodice, waiting while Grizel carefully laced it up the back with gold ribbon. She sat carefully, letting her tiring woman brush out her long rich chestnut brown hair. It would be worn loose, attesting to her virginity. A gold ribbon embroidered with tiny glittering bits of gold quartz was fastened about her forehead to hold her tresses in place. Maggie stood and took the soft leather gloves Grizel handed her. They would be riding to the kirk. Her servant slipped a fur cape about her shoulders.

"Yer ready," Grizel said.

Maggie descended into the great hall where the men of her family awaited her. Her grandfather was dressed in a long, dark brown velvet coat with full-puffed sleeves, and a large fur collar. She smiled at him, but then her gaze went to her husband, and her eyes widened with both approval and surprise. If as Grizel had said, she was fine enough to appear at the king's court, then so was Lord Fingal Stewart.

CHAPTER 6

She had always thought him passing fair for a man, but looking at him now, she realized how handsome he truly was. At five feet ten inches, she was considered extremely tall for a woman, but he topped her by at least half a foot. His thick wavy black hair was cropped short. His gray eyes looked out at her from beneath thick bushy black eyebrows. He had a long face with an aquiline nose, and while his mouth was big and thin, when he smiled it changed the severity of his countenance. He smiled at her now, and Maggie smiled back.

"Ye are beautiful, madam," he gallantly told her, taking her hand up and kissing it.

"As are ye, my lord," she said, admiring his deep green velvet doublet with its bit of gold embroidery, padded sleeves, and fur cuffs. He had matching slashed breeches, silk stockings that showed his shapely calves, and embroidered shoes.

"Archie seems to have some magic that grants him proper garments for me when the occasion demands it," Fingal Stewart answered. He had fully expected to wear the black and brown canions he wore to court. He tucked her hand into his arm.

"Can we get to the kirk for the blessing?" the old laird asked impatiently.

"I could do it here, Brother," Father David Kerr said.

"Nay! I want the blessing pronounced in the kirk," Dugald Kerr replied. "The kirk is full of Kerrs now waiting for this."

"We should not keep them waiting another minute then, my lord," Fingal Stewart said. Then he turned to Maggie and said mischievously, "Do ye want to race?"

She laughed loudly. "Nay, my lord. We shall proceed through the village upon our mounts at a docile pace as is suitable for this day."

In the courtyard a fine chestnut gelding and a cream-colored mare with a dark mane and tail stood waiting patiently. Lord Stewart lifted Maggie onto the mare, waiting while she pulled on her riding gloves and adjusted her skirts; she did not ride astride this day. Then he swung himself up on the gelding next to the laird and the priest, who were already mounted. Slowly they descended the hill path and into the village. The street was lined with villagers who then fell in behind the riders escorting them.

The priest hurried into the church building with the villagers behind him eager to find places among the keep's servants where they too might watch the ceremony. Lord Stewart lifted Maggie from her saddle. When her feet had touched the ground, she found herself flanked by her grandfather on one side of her and Fingal Stewart on the other. Together the two men escorted her into the kirk and up the aisle where Father David Kerr stood awaiting them. Without a single word, Dugald Kerr, laird of Brae Aisir, placed his granddaughter's hand into the hand of Lord Fingal Stewart. Then he stepped back and aside to watch the proceedings as Edmund Kerr glared, angry to have been foiled.

"Kneel," the priest said. When they had, he pronounced the church's blessing upon the union of Margaret Jean Kerr of Brae Aisir and Lord Fingal David Stewart of Torra. A hand rested upon the head of the bride and of the groom as he spoke. Then Mass was celebrated for all within the small kirk. When it concluded, David Kerr announced, "Fingal Stewart and Maggie Kerr are now man and wife in the eyes of the church as well as the laws of Scotland."

"Huzzah! Huzzah! Huzzah!" those within the church shouted with one voice.

"Long life and many bairns to our Maggie and her man!"

They arose from the velvet-cushioned kneelers. Fin swept Maggie into his arms and kissed her quite thoroughly to the delight of the clansmen and women. Then they hurried from the church together, the old laird coming behind them, accepting the congratulations of his folk. Rosy with blushes, Maggie was already seated upon her mare.

Fin aided Dugald Kerr to clamber upon his horse, then mounted his own animal, and they returned to the keep, the Netherdale Kerrs and the village coming behind them.

In the courtyard Maggie and Fin greeted each Kerr, giving them a small but useful gift; honing stones for the men, a small basket of colored threads for the women, and a sugar plum for each child. There were ale and sweet cakes for everyone. A health was drunk to the bride, the groom, and the laird. Then the clan folk departed back to their own cottages, allowing the wedding party to reenter the hall where the celebratory feast would now be enjoyed by the family and its retainers.

It was midafternoon now. The day had cleared. As the sun set and the fires blazed in the hall hearths, the food was brought forth to the high board. Fresh trout and salmon were served on platters of peppery wild cress. This was followed by a roasted goose, a leg of lamb, a ham, and a rabbit stew with tiny onions and sliced carrots in a rich brown gravy flavored with red wine. There was a bowl of late peas from the kitchen garden, and some lettuces braised in white wine along with fresh bread served with both butter and two cheeses. The cups, studded with green agate, were filled with dark red wine that tasted sweet to Maggie's tongue.

Below the high board the men-at-arms and the family's retainers enjoyed trout, ham, rabbit stew, bread, and cheese, while their cups were never empty of the laird's good ale. There was much camaraderie and laughter between the trestles, for the men of Brae Aisir and Lord Stewart's men were now one and the same.

Lord Edmund glowered out over the small assembly. He had lost his chance to gain the whole of the Aisir nam Breug today. But there was always tomorrow. Maggie could prove infertile. She might die in childbed or birth only daughters. Discord could be sewn among the Kerr clan folk when old Dugald died. Did the Kerrs really want a Stewart overlord and master? Despite his son's warning, Edmund Kerr wasn't ready to yet concede his loss. His fist tightened about the stem of his goblet, and his lips narrowed.

"We're leaving immediately on the morrow," Rafe Kerr said quietly to his sire. "The head groom in the stable says there's a storm coming in another day or two. I'd just as soon be home in Netherdale Hall when it does."

"Aye," his father agreed. "No need for us to remain here any longer. My cousin will be glad to see the back of me, I'm certain."

Rafe laughed. "Aye, Da, he will, 'tis truth. Old Dugald doesn't like you at all. He told me he holds you responsible for not telling him that Glynis was frail."

"I had hoped my half sister would produce an heir for Brae Aisir whom I would one day influence and match with one of my daughters," Edmund Kerr said.

"So you've meant to have it all along, Da, have you?" Rafe was surprised, but then once his father got an idea he liked stuck in his head, it was difficult, if not impossible, to move him in another direction. He was his father's heir, and he certainly did not want the entire responsibility of the Aisir nam Breug to fall upon him. Their eight miles were enough for him. His father hadn't managed his responsibility in years. It was Rafe who had overseen their part of the pass since he was sixteen. He was now past thirty. Some years were more difficult than others depending on whether England and Scotland were quarreling. And if they were, keeping the Aisir nam Breug safe was harder.

But from the looks of Lord Stewart, his cousin's bridegroom was a strong man and would sire strong sons on Maggie. She was nothing like her mother had been. Glynis Kerr had been beautiful, but a wise man would have seen she was frail. Sadly, Dugald Kerr's son was not wise, and Rafe was frankly amazed she had lived to birth three bairns despite the fact the only one surviving was a lass. Dugald Kerr had blamed Edmund Kerr for not pointing out that Glynis was delicate, and for the sake of them all discouraging the match between his half sister and the laird's son. But Dugald had had three sons then, and several other grandchildren. Who could have anticipated all that had happened, and that a lass would end up the last of the Kerrs of Brae Aisir?

"Ye hae a serious look about ye, lad," the laird said. " 'Tis a happy occasion we celebrate today. Do ye have a wife?"

"Aye, sir, I do. And two little lads and two little lasses," Rafe said with a smile.

"Then the succession of yer family is assured," the laird remarked. "I hope by this time next year the succession of ours is as well."

"The bairn won't be a Kerr," Edmund said meanly.

"What matter?" Dugald snapped back. "The bairn will have *my* blood. No family's male line goes on forever, ye sour fool! Yers will end one day too. The name of Stewart is a proud and noble one. Can I complain that one of that royal line will take my place eventually, Edmund? I know that Fin will keep our portion of the pass safe, and so will his sons and sons' sons. And yer Rafe is a reasonable man. He will work well with my granddaughter heiress's husband. Kerr and Stewart together keeping the Aisir nam Breug as it has always been. A safe traverse for honest travelers. Now shut yer mouth, and cease yer carping, for what's done is done, and what is, is."

Rafe hid his smile. He knew of no other who would dare to speak with his father in such a manner.

The laird's piper now came into the hall and began to play. Maggie and Fin danced a country wedding dance in the space between the high board and the trestle tables. It was a simple stately dance that had been executed for centuries in Scottish halls throughout the land. Fin's arm about Maggie, they moved slowly and sensuously to the deep rhythm the piper, a drummer, and a clansman playing upon a flute performed.

Her head back against his shoulder, she looked up into his handsome face and recognized the look of longing upon it. Maggie's heart beat a little faster. Her velvet skirts swirled about them as they danced. He lifted her up and swung her about. His eyes never left her face, and she found she was unable to turn away from him though her cheeks grew pink. And then as the dance slowly came to an end, Fin bent to brush her lips with his. Maggie sighed audibly, then blushed with the realization of it. He smiled down into her face and led her back to the high board. To her surprise, she found herself breathless.

Then Clennon Kerr and Iver Leslie arose to dance amid two crossed swords in the same expanse. In their stocking feet they stepped agilely and gracefully between the sharp blades as the music grew more and more spritely. The efforts of the dancers were much appreciated by the onlookers. As the two men finished, those at the trestles arose, clapping and shouting their approval. Another round of ale was suggested. When the kegs ran dry, the evening would end for the guests.

Grizel arose from her place at a trestle and slipped up to the high board to whisper in her mistress's ear. Maggie nodded. She leaned over, saying to her grandfather, "I shall depart the hall now, Grandsire." He nodded silently. Maggie reached out to touch the arm of her cousin Rafe. "I know you will leave even before dawn," she said to him. "Thank you for coming. I wish you a safe passage home, Rafe Kerr."

"And I wish you and Fin happiness and many sons, Cousin," he replied. "I'll tell Da you bid him farewell. As you can see, he is in his cups now." His head nodded to Lord Edmund, who had fallen asleep still clutching his goblet, which was now empty.

Maggie couldn't help but smile. "His head will hurt the whole way home," she said. "I doubt he'll come again soon to Brae Aisir."

Rafe chuckled wickedly as she arose and hurried from the hall to the cheers of the men-at-arms who watched her go. Rafe spoke now to Fingal Stewart. "It's unlikely I'll see you on the morrow, my lord, so I will bid you farewell tonight. For the sake of the Aisir nam Breug, put no trust in my father. He's a devious man, and he would control the entire traverse. He will use any means to gain his way, I fear. If it seems disloyal to you that I speak thusly, know that my concern is for the Aisir nam Breug and our family's safety. The two families working together to maintain and protect the pass over the centuries has kept it safe and free of political influence. But we need both families in this endeavor. I am not disloyal, and will attempt to keep my father's meddling to a minimum, but he is still Lord of Netherdale, and I can only do so much. So beware of him, and his schemes," Rafe Kerr concluded.

"I understand," Lord Stewart replied, and he held out his hand to Rafe, who took and shook it. "Thank ye."

"I wish you happiness, and strong sons," Rafe replied. "And while I see a gleam of eagerness in your eye, you must wait a while longer. Brides need time to prepare themselves for the first coming of their husband. A bit more wine may be in order."

The two men grinned companionably at each other.

Upstairs, however, Maggie had been divested of her wedding finery, and she now sat quietly as Grizel brushed her mistress's long chestnut hair. "Ye were a beautiful bride," Grizel said fondly.

"I ache in every joint," Maggie complained. "My shoulders and arms are so painful, and yet I have fought with my claymore before."

"Not as hard as ye did this day," Grizel responded. "Ye were fierce, lass."

"But he overcame me," Maggie said as she sat while her tiring woman slicked the brush through her thick hair. "I've never been overcome before. Am I really a good swordswoman, or have my opponents been allowing me to win to humor me?"

"Nay, nay," Grizel responded. "No one at Brae Aisir has been yer equal until today, my bairn. But did ye really want to be victorious over him? He did not crow with his triumph, for he has too much respect for ye."

"But he won," Maggie said again.

"Aye, he did. He was tired of the contest, and did not wish to blood ye. He simply knocked the claymore from yer grasp, lass, but I could not say that he overcame ye." She gave her young mistress a mischievous grin.

"Nay, he didn't, did he?" Maggie suddenly felt better about the day's events. She grinned back at Grizel and chuckled.

"But dinna torment him about it, lass," Grizel advised the younger woman. "Sometimes 'tis better to allow a man to think he has the upper hand. And this is yer wedding night. Certainly ye dinna want to quarrel with yer lord." She had finished brushing Maggie's long tresses. Putting the hairbrush aside, she said, "Time to get into yer bed now. I'll be returning to the hall to tell him yer waiting." She helped the girl into bed, plumping the pillows up behind her. Then Grizel bent and kissed Maggie's cheek. "May ye have many healthy sons, my bairn," she said, and turning, she hurried from the bedchamber, closing the door firmly behind her.

Maggie sat almost frozen, her heart beating faster, it seemed, than it usually did. She was very aware of the ache in her shoulders, neck, and arms. More than anything else she wanted a good night's sleep. She wouldn't get it, of course. *He* would come, and they had one more duty to perform this night for the good of Brae Aisir. Her grandfather would want the bloodied sheet proving her virtue to fly from the roof come the morrow.

It was going to hurt. That much she knew for she had heard enough of the servant lasses complain of their first time with a man. But what was it *really* like to be with a man? Was there pleasure after the pain? She didn't know enough about what was to transpire between her *husband* — God's toenail, that word sounded so strange in her mouth and to her ears — and herself. She knew he would cover her body with his and that his cock would find an entry into her body. What more to it was there? Well, she supposed it was as much as many lasses knew, but bloody hell she wished she could avoid it all tonight and just sleep her aching muscles away. He had been a fierce opponent today, and he had given her no quarter at all other than avoiding wounding her.

Grizel reached the hall, and going to the high board murmured in Lord Stewart's ear, "Yer bride awaits ye, my lord." Then she returned to her place at the trestles.

Fin nodded, and leaning over so Dugald Kerr and Rafe Kerr might hear him said, "Good night, my lord, Rafe." Then he arose, and stepping down, made his way from the hall. About him the men-at-arms chuckled softly, and nodded to one another, smiling. Each man had the single thought in his head. Brae Aisir would now be safe. Fingal Stewart would do his duty tonight, and Mad Maggie would birth a future generation for them. They had waited a long time for this moment to come.

He sprinted up the stairs, then stopped suddenly. Where would she be? In his chamber? In hers? Then he heard Archie's voice.

"I'll help ye undress, my lord. Grizel says yer wife awaits ye in her chamber."

Fin breathed a sigh of relief. What a fool he would have looked going from door to door seeking Maggie. He stepped into his own chamber, and with Archie's aid stripped off his wedding finery. "Should I ask where these garments came from?" he said dryly as he pulled off his doublet.

"Honestly come by, my lord, I swear it," his serving man assured his master. He handed him a rag with which to wash. Lord Stewart had bathed fully after the challenge.

Fin washed himself and scrubbed his teeth with the rag. He debated whether to wear the white cotton nightshirt. Probably best he wear it into her bedchamber tonight as she was hardly used to the naked male form. He didn't want her shrieking with fright, and he would have to go through the narrow corridor both coming and going. He turned to go to the door, but Archie's hand stopped him.

"Nay, my lord, this way," the serving man said, and he opened a small curved top door in the wall that Fin had not noticed before, so well was it hidden in the paneling. "Press the carved rose on the other side when you wish to return to your own chamber," Archie murmured in a low voice.

Lord Stewart stepped through into another bedchamber. He turned to carefully close the door behind him, seeking and finding the rose first. The room was dim but for a fire in the hearth, and a taperstick on a small table next to the bed where Maggie now sat up in her bed, straight as a poker, the look on her face a combination of nerves and fear.

Maggie had stiffened as the wee door had swung open and her husband stepped through into the chamber. When he turned to come towards the bed, she swallowed hard.

Fin sat down on the edge of the bed. "Well, madam," he said, "here we are at last as God, the king, and the laws of Scotland would have us."

"I am ready to do my duty," Maggie said primly.

Fin laughed. "Oh, Maggie mine," he

replied, "it may be a duty we do for Brae Aisir, but I want it to be a pleasurable duty for us both."

"How many women have you loved?" she asked, surprising him.

"I have loved none, but I have *made love* to enough to know what is pleasing to lovers," he said. "There are men who believe a woman's body is for their pleasure alone. They take what they want from women and care nothing but for their own enjoyment. I have learned that a man's greatest pleasure comes from giving his woman pleasure too. You are a virgin, of course. Tell me what you know of lovemaking so I may correct the misconceptions first, and then add to your knowledge."

"Could we not just do what needs doing, my lord?" she asked nervously. "I ache in every joint from today's challenge, and want nothing more than sleep." Her cheeks were pink at having said the blunt words just spoken.

Fingal Stewart laughed aloud. "Oh, Maggie mine," he said, "never have I known a woman of such candor as ye are. But what we do this night is more than just a duty." Reaching out, he took her hand in his. It was cold, but her slender fingers curled about his. That was good, he thought. "You aren't afraid of me, are you?" he asked her.

"Nay," she responded. "I know ye now and believe ye to be a good man."

"Are ye afraid of the coupling?" he queried.

"Nay!" Maggie quickly said. Then blushing, she admitted, "Mayhap a little, but only because I am not certain what is expected of me." She sighed. "I do not like being so wretchedly ignorant, my lord."

"Ye must trust me, Maggie mine," he said, "and I have learned these past months that your trust is not easily or quickly given."

"To not be in control of my life is difficult, my lord. I know these are words a man does not often hear from the lips of a woman, but I trust you enough to utter them to you without fear of a beating."

"I will never beat you, my lady wife. A man who beats a woman is admitting his own defeat, and I have never admitted defeat in all my life. Now we both know what needs doing this night, and we shall do it. Then we shall sleep, for I tell you truly that my body aches even more than yers. Ye were not an easy opponent to overcome, Maggie mine." He smiled warmly at her as he spoke.

The words came out before she might stop them. "Ye dinna beat me, my lord."

"I disarmed ye, lass," he replied with a grin, appreciating the fine line of distinction she had drawn and not in the least offended. "And then yer grandsire declared me the victor. Do ye really want to disagree with the old man?"

"And break his heart?" she replied. "Nay, I do not. But ye did not really beat me, my lord. My silence allowed ye the victory, but I am not unhappy with the outcome."

"I am very relieved to hear it, lass," he told her softly. Then he brushed the back of her hand with his lips, slowly kissing each finger upon it. He turned the hand over and placed a deep kiss upon her palm as he looked into her lovely face.

Maggie's hazel eyes grew wide with surprise as she felt a ripple of excitement race through her. She had never known the palm of one's hand could be so sensitive.

"Take off yer night garment," Fin's voice instructed quietly, his eyes meeting hers.

"Will ye take off yers?" she countered, her heart beginning to thump in her ears.

In response, he loosed her hand and pulled his night garb off, tossing it carelessly to the floor. "Turnabout is fair play, madam," he told her.

Unwilling to play the shrinking virgin, Maggie yanked her gown over her head and tossed it bravely onto the floor next to his, but she grasped the coverlet up with one hand to cover her naked breasts, not daring to look at him now.

Then to her surprise Fin stood up. "Look at me," he said to her. "Look and see how a man is fashioned. If you have questions, I will answer them."

This certainly had to be the oddest wedding night any couple had ever had, Maggie considered. Then, raising her gaze, she looked at the naked man before her. He was surely the most magnificent male creature ever created, she decided, despite her lack of sources for comparison. Oh, she had seen men in the fields naked from the waist up. She had seen others, their lower torsos wrapped in linens as they labored on the few hot days of summer. She had even seen glimpses of male buttocks as they eagerly used a lass in the hay or the hedges. But never had she seen a fully naked man, or one of such perfection.

He was wonderfully tall, and his limbs were in perfect proportion to his trunk. His arms, his chest, and his back were muscled, but not overly so. His calves were exceedingly shapely, his thighs strong. He was not a hairy man like some she had seen. There was the lightest covering of down on his legs and arms. His broad chest, however, was smooth. His buttocks were firm, and she was certain she saw a dimple where his spine split the flesh into twin moons. His feet were large, suiting his size. A thick thatch of black curls sprang forth from his mons. His manhood hung long and relaxed amid it. It didn't look at all particularly dangerous, Maggie thought. In fact it seemed rather indifferent. What if her body didn't excite it? After all, he had said he was marrying her because the king had told him to wed her. It had hardly been a flattering commentary.

Fin had turned himself slowly so she might observe him at her leisure in his entirety. Now he held out his hand to her. "Come, madam," he said. "Ye've now seen me. I would see ye." He gently peeled the coverlet from her hand and drew her forth from the bed onto her feet to stand where he might view her as freely and as frankly as she had viewed him. She was statuesque for a woman, taller than many men, but he still towered over her. She was beautifully formed with shapely arms and legs, a light ripple of muscle across her smooth shoulders that eased into a long back. Her buttocks were surprisingly round and plump. He wanted to kneel then and there to nip at

210

them, but he didn't. Her breasts were round but not overly large. The nipples upon them could be called dainty. Her slim torso boasted a narrow waist that flowed into well-proportioned hips and trim, but firm, thighs. Her mons was covered in chestnut-colored curls, the hue of which matched her long hair. Unlike some women, she did not pluck her curls. His eyes fell at last to her feet, which were slender and long in keeping with her height.

"Yer a beautiful lass," Fin finally said.

Maggie colored. She had hardly breathed as his gray eyes had slowly explored her female form. But now unable to help herself, she sneezed.

"Into bed with ye, lass," he said, quickly pushing her toward the furniture in question and as swiftly climbing in next to her.

It had been done so quickly, Maggie didn't have time to consider it, but suddenly she was lying side by side with this man who was her husband. He put his arms about her, and she gave a little cry of surprise. *"Oh!"* He was wrapped about her, and the sensation of his flesh touching her flesh was amazing to her.

"Yer chilled," he said with understatement. " 'Twas selfish of me to keep ye from our warm bed, feasting myself on yer fair form, Maggie mine," he apologized.

"Yer my husband, and ye may do as ye please with me," Maggie said.

"Nay," he replied, surprising her. "It was thoughtless, lass, but yer so beautiful."

"So are ye," she murmured back. She was beginning to feel warm again.

Fin chuckled. "I dinna think I've ever been called beautiful, but I thank ye."

His arms tightened about her, and he kissed the top of her head.

Maggie winced.

"What is it?" His voice was filled with concern.

"If ye might not hold me so tightly, my lord," she said to him. "My neck and shoulders really do ache. I don't ever recall being so sore."

He loosened his grip upon her. " 'Tis difficult not to hold ye tightly, lass," he admitted to her. "It seems as if I've waited forever to hold ye."

"Ye but came to Brae Aisir less than four months ago, my lord," she said.

"But I knew then ye were to be my wife, and when I saw ye, how could I not want to hold ye in my arms?" Fin felt her firm young body cradled against him, and a frisson of desire raced down his spine. He knew what was expected of them that night, and she knew too, but he didn't want this first experience with him to be unpleasant. And he realized that until Maggie was with child, he would be expected to be with her each and every night but for a few. He wanted to prepare her for what was to come, and he wanted her content when it was over. Whether her passions could be fully engaged by him he didn't know, but their couplings should be enjoyable, and she should not dread them.

Could they love each other? Did such a thing as love even exist? Was it possible for them to find it together? Fingal Stewart really had no answers to his own questions. But he did know if they liked and respected each other, if they could enjoy the coupling of their bodies and produce bairns for Brae Aisir, the marriage would be a good one. It was the best he could hope for now. The time for talk had ended.

"My lord," she began, but he stopped her mouth with a quick kiss.

"Enough, lass. Let me lead ye, Maggie mine. And while it pleases me to hear ye call me *my lord* in public, in private I would prefer ye spoke my name." His lips met hers once again in a deep passionate kiss.

Maggie almost swooned with the sweet pressure of his mouth on hers. She didn't know if she would ever love him. Was love even real? But a man who kissed her as he was now kissing her certainly could be liked. She kissed him back, feeling his big palm cupping her head as his lips worked against hers. She felt a need to open her own lips to him, and his tongue slid between them to touch, to caress her tongue. Maggie shivered, for she had never imagined such a thing. It was exciting, thrilling, and without her even being aware of it at first, her tongue caressed his back.

When she realized what she was doing, Maggie wasn't certain she should be shocked by her own behavior, but Fin certainly didn't seem to mind. Indeed, he seemed to encourage her actions. Her heart jumped in her chest when his other hand fastened itself about one of her buttocks to bring their bodies into seriously close proximity. The warm hand on her bottom made her briefly faint with excitement. The sensation of their bodies, breast to chest, belly to belly, thigh to thigh, caused her to pull her head away from his delicious kisses, gasping with pleasurable shock. *"Oh my!"* she whispered. The feel of his skin against hers, the scent of him in her nostrils, was utterly and amazingly intoxicating. "I don't know what to do," she said, softly surprised by the sound of her own voice, and that she was able to speak at all.

"Nay, Maggie mine, remember that I will lead ye tonight," Fin said as he now laid her back among the pillows. He sighed audibly. "Ye have the most delicious mouth, love. I could kiss ye all night long but that we have other business to attend to first." His fingers brushed against one of her breasts. Then bending, he ran his tongue slowly between the two round globes. "These are two sweet fruits to be treasured," he told her.

His fingers brushed a breast, slipping beneath it to cup it in his hand.

No one had ever touched her breasts. For that matter, no man had ever touched her body at all. Maggie wasn't a simpleton. She knew he was beginning to make love to her, but the reality compared to the servant lasses' gossip was totally different. She hadn't known her heart would beat so quickly, or that ripples of ice would race down her spine followed by a fiery heat that made her want to cry out. Everything he was doing to her was unfamiliar, but it was wonderful. She heard herself saying to him, "I know ye must lead me, my lord, but instinct makes me want to do something other than lie like a log."

"Let yer instinct be yer guide, lass," he

215

told her. Then his dark head dipped to take one of her nipples into his mouth.

"*Sweet Jesu!*" Maggie cried softly. Her fingers dug into his shoulders as she felt the tug of his lips on her breast because at the same time she had felt a tug in her nether regions. How was this even possible? But as he suckled on her, the sensation didn't go away. Indeed, it increased her rising excitement. She sighed, her delight obvious to him.

He released the nipple and began to press kisses down her torso. He could feel her body quivering beneath his mouth, but she had shown him no fear to his actions so far. She would naturally have a virgin's anxious moments, but so far she was taking to his mouth and hands easily. He ceased his kissing and lay back. She needed to see the havoc she was causing to his body.

"Dinna stop," she said softly. "I like what yer doing."

"I like it too," he replied, "but ye have wanted to participate in our first passion, so I shall instruct ye in what to do, Maggie mine. Sit up and touch my cock. I know ye have not touched one before. This one will pierce yer maidenhead soon, and afterwards it will find its home in yer sweet sheath. It will water yer hidden garden and give ye my

216

seed. Touch it, and know it, love. It is more fearful of the advantage ye will soon hold over it than ye can be of its small power in releasing yer virginity."

She sat up, amazed to see the formerly lean and lank flesh was swollen hard. Reaching out, she wrapped her hand about it, surprised to see that her fingers did not quite meet. Its former length was even longer now. 'Twas a most impressive weapon indeed.

Releasing it, she let her fingers stroke it briefly, then reached beneath to cup his pouch in her warm palm. "Yer balls are cold to my touch," she said to him. "Should they not be heated with yer lust as yer cock is, my lord?"

"Ye must call me Fin, Maggie mine. I know not why a man's balls are chill, but they always are. 'Tis a mystery." He was close to flinging himself atop her, for the hand now playing with him had set his blood aboil.

She nodded as her fingers teased innocently at him. "Yer cock is quite upstanding now, my . . . Fin." She gave it a little squeeze that almost destroyed him.

"Aye, it is. I think we must now consider the removal of yer maidenhead," he replied in what sounded like a calm voice. He gently pushed her back as she released her hold on his manhood. Then he began kissing her again as his hand stroked her torso, moving slowly lower and lower until he reached the nest of chestnut curls. He crushed her mons gently but firmly several times as she gasped with surprise into his mouth. A single finger ran along the slip separating her nether lips, pressing through them to find her little love bud. Fin was pleased to find she was already moist with her rising desire.

He had not been wrong. She was going to be a passionate woman.

Maggie lay as still as a doe in the brush waiting for what was going to come next.

When his finger touched a hitherto unknown place between her nether lips and began to worry it, gently at first, and then with more urgency, she cried out in surprise. He silenced her with more kisses as the tip of that terrible finger played harder. Her head spun, and when a burst of utter pleasure overcame her, she pulled from him, crying out again. "*Sweet Jesu!* No more, I beg ye. 'Tis too delicious."

He did not answer her, instead stroking her flesh into ease, and then moving lower.

Maggie was tightly shut to him. His finger tenderly coaxed the flesh barely enough to begin the gentle pressure that would open her first to his finger, and then to his manhood.

Fin felt her body begin to resist him. "Nah, nah, sweetheart, ye need to be readied for what is to come," he murmured to her.

God's toenail! Why didn't he just mount her and be done with it? Maggie wondered to herself. It had to be better than all this anticipation he was causing to build up within her. She tried to be at ease, and felt the tip of his finger slip into her. *"Oh!"*

Again he said nothing. Instead, he pushed his finger to the second joint.

"Oh!"

And finally Fin sheathed the digit in its entirety. He let it remain there so she might get used to the pressure of it. Then he began a slow rhythm with the finger, moving it back and forth. He was painfully aware as he did so of the ache in his own cock.

"Ohh!" Maggie half whispered. Then she felt herself relaxing and enjoying his sensuous actions. She wanted more. To her great surprise, she realized a primitive instinct made her want that big cock of his pushing inside her. Was she wanton? Or was it natural for a wife to desire her husband so greatly? "Fuck me," she whispered. "Not just with your finger, Fin. I am ready to take

you within me. *Please!*"

The invitation was more than welcome. It was a relief, for his cock was throbbing mightily. Now he needed to take her without spilling his seed too quickly. Nudging her thighs apart with a knee, he covered her body with his. Slowly he guided his aching need into her. First its head, then inch by slow inch until he reached the barrier of her innocence. It was tight, and she winced visibly as his manhood touched it. There was only one way of doing this, Fin knew. Looking into her face, he saw her eyes were squeezed tightly shut. He almost smiled with the sweetness of it. "I'm sorry, lass," he told her, pulling back slightly, then driving himself fully into her sheath.

The shock of it, the burning pain that filled her, caused Maggie to scream. She began to beat at him, her fists thrashing beneath him in an attempt to dislodge him.

And when she couldn't, Maggie, to her embarrassment, began to cry.

Fin kissed the tears from her cheeks, murmuring soothing sounds. " 'Tis done now and 'twill not hurt ever again, Maggie mine," he assured her. Did no one tell her it would hurt? Her maidenhead had been lodged tightly. He continued kissing her tears, which, to his relief, had now ceased.

He kept himself very still for a few brief moments.

"I knew it would hurt," she whispered, "but not like it did. Are we done?" She did not open her eyes to look at him.

Fin laughed softly, brushing her lips with his. "Nay, love, we've but begun." Then he began to move gently upon her, struggling to hold back the explosion of passion that was threatening to overcome him.

The pain had disappeared almost as quickly as it had come. Now the sensation of his cock thick and hot within her engulfed Maggie. Her whole body seemed to be deluged with sensation as he thrust to and fro. She was overwhelmed with languor. Her body, so tense but a few short moments ago, was alive with a plethora of new sensations.

She could divine that he was being careful, gentle with her. Would another man have been so? She couldn't imagine Ewan Hay taking such care with her.

Maggie suddenly wrapped her arms about Fin, drawing him closer to her. His rhythm began to increase. His strength made her absolutely breathless with what she suddenly realized was her own excitement. *"Yes!"* she breathed into his ear.

Fin groaned as her hot breath whispered against his flesh. He wanted her to know some pleasure from this first coupling, but it was becoming more and more difficult to hold back the lust boiling inside him. Then he heard her make a small mewling sound, and looking at her face, he saw the touch of ecstasy glowing. "Aah, Maggie mine," he cried out as his body stiffened, then jerked hard several times.

Somewhere in the delicious haze that had briefly overcome her Maggie felt his cock spasming, and she knew he was releasing his seed into her. Would it take root tonight, or would they have more nights to create an heir for Brae Aisir? She hoped the latter as he fell away from her, lying upon his back and breathing hard.

"I meant for ye to have more pleasure," he said, his tone filled with regret. "I wanted yer first time in my arms to be something ye would remember, but God's toenail, lass, I was like a lad unable to control my lust for ye."

"But I liked it, Fin," Maggie told him. "Except, of course, for the pain. Ye made me feel as I never had before. I know I will enjoy our future couplings."

He laughed low, rolling onto his side to look at her. "Ye found a bit of delight, for I saw it momentarily in yer face," he told her. "But one day perhaps I will be able to make ye cry out with joy as we couple. I want that for ye, Maggie mine. I never cared about it with the women I used to slack my lust. Their bodies were for my delectation. I paid for them, and while I liked giving them pleasure, it didn't matter if it was nothing more than a quick coupling. But with ye, my wife, 'tis different. I want perfection for ye, and I shall keep trying to attain it until I can give it to ye." Leaning over, he kissed her mouth, pleased that she eagerly kissed him back.

She was surprised by his revelation. Was it possible if she used her body to please him that she would hold a certain small power over him? He had said something similar earlier, but she had not understood it then. Now she thought she did. Reaching out, she caressed his face. "Ye were careful with me, and I thank ye for it."

"We are wed until death," he responded. "I want us content with that. I want our bairns to grow to man- and womanhood in a happy home with parents who honor and respect each other. Had I simply satisfied my lust, ye should not have enjoyed this first coupling. Ye might have grown to fear our couplings, and I didn't want that to happen."

"I will not fear them now," Maggie reassured him. "Will ye mount me again tonight? I still ache from our contest today, but I should not mind at all if ye wished to have me once again."

Fin laughed again. Would he ever grow used to Maggie's candid tongue? And it had proved a delicious tongue. Eventually he would teach that facile little tongue new uses that would surely surprise her at first. "Nay," he said. "The deed has been done. On other nights I will enjoy making love to ye the night long, but tonight I think we both could use our rest. Look beneath ye, lass, and see the proof yer grandsire will be proud to display come the morrow."

Maggie shifted herself, and was astounded to see beneath her the bloody stain of her virginity now turning brown upon the fine linen sheet. And she could see her thighs were smeared with dried blood too. She fixed her gaze on Fin. "Aye, we have done well, my lord, and Grandsire will not be shamed."

He arose from her bed, gathering up their two night garments. Handing her hers, he put on his. Then he climbed back into bed with Maggie.

"Ye are not returning to yer own bed?" Many men preferred visiting their wives, and then sleeping in their own beds.

"Tonight I would be with ye," he said as he gathered her into his arms. The delicious feel of her bottom pushing into him was intoxicating. Reaching around, he captured one of her breasts, and burying his face into her scented hair, sighed contentedly. Very quickly he was snoring lightly.

Maggie, however, remained awake a bit longer digesting this evening. This man she had been ordered to wed was turning out to be a better bargain than she had ever anticipated or even imagined. He was intelligent, and he was swiftly learning the ways of the Aisir nam Breug. He had quickly settled into the keep, and he had been easily accepted by all. The Kerr clan folk were usually not so quick to countenance strangers, but they had taken to Fingal Stewart as if he were one of them for all his life.

She snuggled against the sleeping man, enjoying the sensation of his hand clasping her breast. The coupling had been good. His restrained passion had opened a whole new world to her. Maggie could not help but wonder what that passion was going to be like when it was fully unleashed. And would she be able to match his ardor? She very much wanted to match it. Aye! She did! Her eyes were growing heavy, but before she fell into a contented sleep, Mad Maggie

Kerr considered that she had never before pondered such a thing. Why was she contemplating it now? The coupling was for the purpose of creating heirs for Brae Aisir. That's what the church taught. There certainly was nothing more to it than that. *Or was there?* She realized as she finally tumbled into sleep that she couldn't wait to find out.

CHAPTER 7

To their mutual surprise they slept late, and no one came to disturb them. Maggie was amazed to find him still in her bed. His eyes were closed, his breathing even. She took the opportunity to look down at him. She had been correct in her observation the past night. He was handsome — not pretty like a lass, but in a masculine way, with his long straight nose, high cheekbones, and long thin mouth. He had shaved his face yesterday, but already a shadowy veil of black beard was beginning to show itself. His eyelashes were certainly thick for a man's, Maggie thought. His eyes suddenly opened, and she found herself staring into molten silver.

"Oh!"

"May I assume ye like what ye observe, madam?" he teased, and the long mouth turned up in a smile.

"Aye, yer a bonnie lad, Fingal Stewart,"

Maggie answered back pertly. She wasn't going to blush and simper like some little fool, although his open eyes had surprised her.

"Yer a bonnie lass," he responded. "We'll make pretty bairns together."

"The sun is way past dawn," she said. "Why did no one come to awaken us?" She made no move to arise from the bed.

"I believe they were being discreet," Fin replied. "They are giving me time to ravage ye again, for all here are eager for an heir." The gray eyes were twinkling.

"Should we do *it* again now?" Maggie asked curiously. " 'Tis morning, and the sun is shining brightly."

"Aye, it is," he said. "But yer newly opened, love. I think we may wait until tonight to continue with our endeavors, madam. Unless, of course, yer feeling particularly lustful for my body," Fin teased her further.

"Yer a fool," she told him, but she laughed.

"Did ye enjoy the coupling?" he asked candidly. She had said last night that she did, but he wanted to be certain now in the light of day that he had not repelled her.

"Aye," she answered him. "I did. After the pain. I must ask ye, husband, for I have no knowledge of these things prior to last night, but there was something more than just the linking of our bodies, Fin. For a brief moment I sensed something I had never felt before. Do ye know what it was? Did ye feel it too?"

" 'Twas pleasure, Maggie mine," he said. "Virgins do not usually have much pleasure, if they have it at all. The sweetness of passion comes with time. As to men, if they are with a lover who pleases them, they too gain delight from their togetherness."

Maggie nodded. "I suppose we should get up. Hopefully the Netherdale Kerrs are already gone into the pass."

Flinging back the coverlet, he climbed from the bed. "I'll see Grizel comes to ye," Fin said as he pressed the little rose carving on the wall. The door sprang open, and he was gone through it, leaving her alone in the bed.

It was almost an hour before Grizel appeared. "Ye look rested," she said brightly.

"His lordship has gone down to the hall. I've had the tub brought to his chamber so ye can bathe before going down. Come along with ye now, my lady." She quickly helped Maggie from the bed, hurrying her through the hidden door and helping her into the tub.

"Now ye just soak a bit while I take the

evidence of yer virtue lost to yer grandsire," she told her mistress before she bustled out, leaving Maggie in the tub.

Returning to her mistress's bedchamber, Grizel pulled back the coverlet and stared down at the stained bed linen. Nodding with satisfaction, she pulled it from the bed. Then she hurried down to the hall, the sheet gathered to her ample bosom. Dugald Kerr was still seated at the high board. He was engaged in conversation with Maggie's new husband. Grizel stepped before the board. "My lord," she said to the laird, curtsying.

Dugald Kerr looked up.

Grizel flung open the sheet to reveal the bloodstain.

The old laird looked, nodded, and then said, "Have Clennon Kerr fly it from the battlements, and tell my granddaughter she has done well."

Grizel curtsied again. "Aye, my lord." Then gathering the linen back up, she left the hall.

"She was braw," Fingal Stewart told the laird.

Dugald Kerr nodded. "Aye, she's always been a brave lass." Then he looked closely at the younger man. "Ye like her, don't ye?"

"Aye, I do," Fingal answered without any hesitation. "She makes me laugh with that sharp tongue of hers. She has no fear of speaking her mind."

"That's why I let her have her way in this matter of marriage," the laird responded. "Maggie has always known what she wants. I suspect if the king hadn't sent ye, and ye had been a lesser man, my granddaughter would still be a maid."

"If the king had sent another?" Fingal asked, curious as to what the laird would say to his query.

"She would have eventually killed him rather than wed him," the old laird said bluntly. "Ye gained her respect quickly, but for the honor of the Kerrs, she had ye meet the challenge she had set forth for all of her suitors. And that has gained ye credibility with our neighbors, particularly as ye beat her."

"We were equal in both races," Fingal said, "and she would not have given up in the swordplay had ye not declared me the victor. I cannot say with complete honesty that I overcame her. I am frankly astounded at her skills."

"Ye disarmed her fairly," Dugald Kerr said. "She is a braw lass, Fingal, but in truth she could hardly stand any longer, let alone wield her claymore. My judgment was a fair one. Maggie knew it too, for if she had disagreed with me, she would have shouted it to the high heavens for all of Scotland, and not just the Borders, to hear."

Fin laughed. "Aye," he agreed with the older man, "she would have."

Upstairs, Maggie soaked in her tub. The water felt wonderful, and the wretched soreness she had felt in her muscles the past night was almost gone as was the soreness between her thighs she had awakened with this morning. Would she be sore each time they coupled? He had promised her there would be no more pain after the first time. Well, she would learn if it was truth tonight, for he had said they would sleep together again each night until she was with child. It was fair.

When she went down to the hall, she found her grandsire alone. "Where is Fin?" she asked him. "And please tell me the Netherdale Kerrs are gone."

Dugald Kerr chuckled. "Aye, at first light, and Edmund complaining as they departed. As for yer husband, he's gone out to make certain the men in the watchtowers have what they need to weather the snowstorm old Tam says is coming."

"How long ago did he leave?" Maggie wanted to know.

"Too long for ye to catch up with him,"

the laird said. "The hall is yer province now, lass."

"Ye know if I don't get out of doors I will suffer for it, Grandsire," Maggie said reasonably. "Once the storm sets in, I will be forced to remain in the hall until it passes."

Dugald Kerr sighed deeply. "Margaret Jean," he said, and she knew when he called her by her full Christian name that it was serious. "The Aisir nam Breug is no longer yers to watch over. That's what yer husband is for, lass. Let him do his duty so he may gain the respect of the men who serve him now. Dinna go trailing after him. If ye would ride out, take a man with ye, but stay away from the pass. Go out and visit the far cottages. 'Tis yer place to see to our clan folk now as the lady of Brae Aisir."

Maggie thought a long moment. As much as she hated to admit to it, to face it, her grandsire was right. The Aisir nam Breug was Fin's obligation now, not hers. A sense of great loss overcame her. She had known with a part of her being that this day would come, yet she had not expected it to really happen. But it had, and she would have to make a new place for herself in the scheme of things. "Yer right, Grandsire," she said. "I'll ride out to the far cottages, and aye, I'll take a few of the men with me."

" 'Tis hard, Maggie lass; I know, for I can see it in yer eyes. But yer a woman, and a woman's place is different from that of a man," Dugald Kerr said. His tone was a kindly one, but Maggie felt a flash of bitterness at those words.

"My sex mattered little these past years when I controlled the traverse for ye, Grandsire. Think if ye will that others thought ye were just indulging me and allowing me to play while it was ye who really held the reins to our heritage. Well, perhaps some did believe it, for there are still enough men in this world who think a woman is not capable of anything other than hearth and bairns, but others knew better. They knew ye lay ill, and I was in charge. The Aisir nam Breug has never been managed better than when I was managing it, so do not, I beg ye, tell me that my place is in the hall at my loom while I wait for my big belly to ripen." Then turning abruptly, Maggie departed the hall.

Dugald Kerr watched her go. She was right, of course, but what did that matter? She was a woman, and the rest of the world would refuse to see her for anything other than that. It saddened him, for he did not want his granddaughter unhappy, but had he died before she wed, their neighbors would have been upon her like a wolf on a lamb.

Out in the stables, Maggie saddled her stallion, calling to Clennon Kerr to bring a few men and ride out with her. Finished, she climbed upon the animal's back and rode him out into the yard.

"Where are we going?" Clennon Kerr asked her.

"To the far cottages. I should see that all is well for the cottagers," Maggie said.

"Take Iver Leslie then," Clennon Kerr replied. "He's nae been that way, and he should have some familiarity with the path. Yer not going to the pass?"

"My husband is there now," Maggie said shortly.

"Aye," Clennon Kerr said. " 'Tis right he should be, my lady."

"Get the men going with me," Maggie told him sharply. "I'll not dally this day, with the coming snows."

The keep's captain said nothing more. He understood why she was in a black mood today, but 'twas past time she took her rightful place as the lady and gave Brae Aisir some bairns. He went off to fetch Iver, calling to several men as he did to get their horses and mount up. Several minutes later, Maggie and her party of men-at-arms rode across the drawbridge and out into the hills.

They rode in silence for some minutes, Iver at Maggie's side. Finally she turned to him, saying, "The cottages we're visiting are at the edge of our lands. We've made them very secure for the inhabitants. They're stone, the windows have thick shutters, the doors are bound in iron, and each of the three dwellings has a small well inside so they may be self-contained in the event of attack. There are no families there. Only men, and three older women who take care of them. They are shepherds, and cattle herders."

"They're helpless in case of attack, however," Iver said.

Maggie laughed. It was a hard sound. "Nay," she told him, "but ye'll see."

The day was fair, but cold. There wasn't a cloud in the bright blue sky, nor was there the faintest puff of wind. They rode for more than an hour, and then Iver saw ahead of them in the distance on the low hills a grouping of three cottages. Maggie sent one of the clansmen ahead to warn the cottagers of her coming.

"The sheep and cattle are now at Brae Aisir, but in the summer these are some of the meadows in which they browse."

"What do these men do when the beasties

are at the keep?" Iver asked, curious.

"They patrol the border between us and our neighbors," Maggie said. "They make repairs to their equipment and warn us of any undue activity in the region."

"Why are we here then?" Iver persisted.

"I'm the lady of the keep," Maggie said. "It's my duty to see to their well-being. The women who look after these clansmen look to me. My visit allows them to know they are not forgotten out here."

Iver nodded. He was admiring of his mistress, although he would have never admitted to such a thing. It wasn't his place to approve or disapprove of her.

Reaching the cottages, they dismounted. A large-boned woman was waiting to greet them. "My lady!" she said, curtsying. "Ye honor us, and with the storm coming."

"Good morrow, Bessy Kerr," Maggie greeted the woman. "I wanted to be certain ye had all ye need for the winter."

"Oh, aye, my lady, everything is in order as you would wish it. Clennon saw our supplies delivered several days ago when Tam told him of this earlier than usual storm. But there is one small difficulty."

"What is that?" Maggie wanted to know.

"Mary's daughter is near her time. 'Tis a first bairn, and Mary desperately wants to be with her, my lady. The lass never told her mam she was almost five months gone when she wed last summer, or Mary would have asked sooner. She learned it from her son-in-law, who brought our supplies, when the bairn was due."

"Can ye manage with just the two of ye?" Maggie asked.

"Oh, aye! Mary's burden is the lightest. She cares for just four lads. We can close up her cottage until the spring when she returns to us. Sorcha and I have more than enough room for two each," Bessy Kerr said cheerfully.

"Tell Mary she can ride back with us," Maggie said.

"Thank ye, my lady!" Bessy curtsied again. Then her eye went to Iver. "And who is this fine laddie?" she asked him.

"Iver Leslie," was the short answer, and he reddened slightly.

"He came with my lord from Edinburgh and is Clennon Kerr's second in command," Maggie explained. "My union with Lord Stewart was blessed yesterday."

Bessy's eyes grew wide. "He overcame ye, my lady? I never thought to see the day when anyone could outrun, outride, and outfight ye, but . . ." she said, hesitating.

" 'Twas past time," Maggie, chuckling,

finished the sentence for Bessy.

Bessy nodded, grinning back at her lady. "Aye," she agreed. "Now, will ye come into my cottage for some cakes and ale?"

"See to the others. I want to show Iver about, and then we'll join ye," Maggie answered the woman. Then looking at her companion she said, "Come along, Iver."

He followed her while she led him about the small settlement, pointing out what he might need to know one day. "Ye still haven't told me why these clan folk of yers are safe in an attack. Aye, the cottages are strong, and the slate roof on each will prevent their being destroyed by fire, but eventually they have to give in," Iver said.

"Nay, they don't," Maggie told him. "In each cottage is a small dovecote. In the event of an attack, three pigeons are released, one from each cote, with a message attached to one of their wee legs. They come home to Brae Aisir entering the keep into their own special cote. There is always someone watching that cote for them. No one has figured out how we so quickly repel an attack on our borders," she laughed. "There are two more places on our lands where cottages with pigeon cotes exist. We'll visit them in the spring, for there is no time today."

Iver nodded. " 'Tis cleverly done," he said.

"I've shown ye all ye need to know here," Maggie told him. "Let's go and get some cakes and ale before we return home. Do ye mind riding pillion with Mary?"

"Nay, I'll take the woman," he said, following his mistress to Bessy's cottage. As he ate a fresh-baked oatcake and drank some good October ale, Iver looked about the cottage. It was a well-kept space, clean and neat, with three rooms. The main one, where the men ate and socialized, was the largest. A second room had space for a row of beds. The third was the smallest, and obviously belonged to Bessy. It had a door that could be locked, and no window. It was all very well thought out, he considered. As he drank his ale and ate the oatcake, Bessy flirted with him.

"Yer a fine strong lad," she said, her hand on his arm. "I wouldn't mind having a bit of a tumble with ye." She grinned up at him.

"Yer a shameless woman," he said low. "Ye've got a houseful of lads to play with, Bessy Kerr."

"Nay, Iver Leslie, I would never swive one of them, for it would make the others jealous, and then I should have to fuck them all. There are few secrets kept in a cottage."

And while the others were engaged in

speaking with their lady, Bessy reached down and gave his manhood a squeeze. "My lads know me, and they'll keep the lady busy while ye and I have a little fun." Bessy gave him a coquettish grin and pulled him from the room.

She was a woman who wasn't going to take no for an answer, and he suspected they wouldn't get away until he had given her what she wanted. He followed Bessy to her small chamber, and when she shut the door, he surprised her by pushing her up against it and giving her a hard kiss. "Very well, lass, let's give ye what ye need so we may be on our way before the snow starts," he said as her hands yanked his breeks down so she might fondle him to a stand. Iver surprised Bessy by his quick reaction to her touch.

"Yer a big man," she said. "Good! It's been months since I've had a good swiving, lad. Now I'll get through the winter."

His hands pushed her skirts up, clamped beneath her big bottom, and lifted her up to impale her on his manhood. Bessy squealed with excitement, wrapping her arms and legs about him as he began to piston her vigorously. Within moments she was moaning into his shoulder, but he seemed not to be tiring. Bessy was astounded by his vigor. She couldn't ever remember a man using her in so lusty and long a manner.

"Tell me when yer ready," he finally growled into her ear.

Bessy was near to fainting with her excitement and satisfaction. She was going to die if he didn't soon stop. *"Now!"* she managed to gasp.

With a deep chuckle Iver released his own pent-up lust, and when it had drained itself into her, he gave her a hearty kiss, squeezed her plump buttock cheeks hard, and set her down again. Then he pulled up his breeks, fastening them.

She clung to him briefly to keep from falling, for at first her legs would not sustain her. "God's toenail, Iver Leslie, I certainly hope I'll see ye again!" she told him enthusiastically. "Yer the first man who's ever truly satisfied me." Bessy smoothed her skirts first, and then her hair. "We had best join the others," she said. "I don't want the lady realizing what we were doing."

But Maggie hadn't noticed the disappearance of her captain and Bessy. She had been too busy speaking with the men who watched over their borders, and giving the latest gossip to Sorcha and Mary. When they were ready to depart, Iver was relieved to see that Mary was not a big woman as was Bessy. Short and slender, she would not tire his horse unduly. He took her up behind him on his horse, and then, giving Bessy a wink, turned to make the ride home to Brae Aisir.

"The storm is coming in early," Maggie noted as the flakes began to fall when they were but halfway home. "I hope my lord gets home safely."

"The wind is coming from the north," Iver said, "but 'tis barely a breeze."

"It will rise later on," Maggie told him. "Look at how small the flakes are. 'Twill be a serious storm, I'm thinking." She pulled up the hood on her cloak and hunched down as she rode. Even with her fur-lined gloves, her hands were cold, her fingers stiffening and making it difficult to hold the reins.

When they finally reached the village, the snow was coming down harder. The land around them was already covered in white. They stopped briefly to let Mary down at her daughter's cottage. It seemed the mother had arrived in the nick of time, for her child had just gone into labor; the village midwife was hurrying up to the door at the same time as the traveler. "Mam!" They heard the girl's cry of relief as Mary rushed into the cottage.

Through the village and up the rise to the keep they rode. As they clomped across the drawbridge, Maggie could see her husband and his men just ahead of them.

She found herself relieved at the sight of Fin dismounting his stallion as she slid quickly from her own mount, tossing the reins to a stable boy as she did. Maggie smiled at him as he turned about. "I was fearful ye would get caught out in the Aisir nam Breug. The storm came earlier. Tam's old bones aren't quite as accurate as they once were."

"Ye went out in this?" he asked.

"There was no snow when we departed for the far cottages," Maggie told him. "I took Iver and several of the men with me. I don't like staying indoors all the time, my lord. And a good thing we went too. We had to bring back one of the women for her daughter's lying-in. Mary arrived just in time. The lass was already in labor."

They walked together into the hall, brushing the snow from themselves as they came. The old laird looked up, relief upon his face.

"Now, Grandsire," Maggie teased him, "certainly ye weren't worried. I've been out in worse than this, and ye know it."

"Of course, I wasn't fearful for ye," Dugald Kerr prevaricated.

Maggie laughed, and going to him planted a kiss on his forehead.

"Sit down, sit down," the laird said to them both. "Well, Fin, how was the pass this day? Was all well?"

"I rode the hills above the Aisir nam Breug and went to the farthest watchtower first. Then we made our way back. All was as it should be, Dugald. The towers were well stocked with food and firewood, and the men were ready for the storm. From my vantage point I could see the Netherdale Kerrs just passing over the border. They did not see me."

"Good, good," Dugald Kerr said, nodding. Then he turned to Maggie.

"The far cottages are supplied for the winter. Clennon saw to it a few days ago. We brought Mary Kerr back with us, as her daughter was ready to deliver her first bairn.

"Bessy and Sorcha assured us they could manage the winter without her. Mary's lass had just gone into labor, and we reached the cottage at the same time Midwife Agnes did. After the storm passes, I'll send to see all went well, and if it did, we'll bring a gift."

"Well," the laird said, "ye've both had a busy day. The meal is ready, and ye'll want an early bed after yer cold ride."

Maggie laughed again. "Grandsire, ye must never go to court, for subtlety is not yer gift, I fear." But she felt her cheek warming as her eye caught Fin's, and he winked wickedly at her.

The wooden trenchers were set upon the high board and the trestles to be filled with hot venison stew. Father David, who usually ate with them, said a blessing. There was bread, butter, and cheese. They ate heartily, washing their food down with a dark red wine. Maggie wanted something sweet after the meal. Grizel fetched her a small dish of stewed apples and pears. The laird's piper came into the hall and played for them. Dugald Kerr, and his younger brother, David, left the high board to play a game of chess.

Maggie arose from her place. "Give me time to bathe lightly," she said, and was gone from the hall.

He watched her go, thinking that although they had but formally consummated their marriage only yesterday, it felt as if he had been with her and at Brae Aisir forever. He looked forward to going upstairs and spending the evening in her bed. He had never seen himself as a married man, but he realized in a burst of clarity that he very much liked the way his life seemed to be progressing. The hall was warm, his belly was full, his bonnie and braw wife was waiting for him. Could a man really ask for more? Standing up, he stretched himself, stepped down from the high board, and left the hall.

"What think ye?" the priest asked his older brother, watching as Fin departed.

"Oddly, they seem well suited," Dugald Kerr said, and he smiled. "He told me he likes her. That's to the good, Davy."

"Does she like him?" the priest said.

"Maggie has said naught to me but that she respects him. She's not a lass who flirted or teased the lads. She's never been in love even a wee bit. But if she respects him, she will be a good wife to him, and she will do her duty by us all," the laird concluded. He moved his knight piece into an attack position.

"I'll pray for them both," David Kerr said as he studied the chessboard, deciding how he would counter his elder sibling's move.

Fingal Stewart had gone up the stairs into the narrow hallway to his own bedchamber. He found Archie waiting for him. His serving man had put out a cloth, a rag, and a basin of hot water with a little cake of soap for his master. He took Lord Stewart's garments and boots as they were removed.

"Will ye want yer night garment, my

lord?" he asked in a bland voice.

"Nay," Fin answered briefly as he quickly washed himself.

"Is there anything more I might do for ye then, my lord?" Archie said.

"Nay, thank ye," came his answer. "Go and see if ye can steal a kiss from Grizel."

Archie chuckled. "She's not an easy woman, my lord," he said. "Good night."

The serving man shut the door behind him and was gone.

Fin smiled at the reply as he pressed the carved rose that opened the door connecting their two chambers. He stepped through into Maggie's bedroom. She was seated cross-legged and naked upon the bed, brushing her long chestnut-colored hair.

Looking up at his entrance, she smiled mischievously at him. "I see we are of one mind," she said, her eyes boldly sweeping over him.

"Aye, I thought it practical," he agreed, climbing into bed with her and taking the brush from her hand as he seated himself behind her. He began to stroke it through her long locks. "I like yer hair," he said. "It smells of flowers." Bending, he kissed her shoulder and nuzzled the curve of her neck. He set the brush aside.

"Ye have hair as black as a raven's wing,"

Maggie replied. "I never knew anyone with such dark hair." She had not ever considered a man would brush her tresses, but she had to admit to herself that she very much liked it. The kiss and nuzzle he gave her set her pulse racing, as did the knowledge that they sat together naked in her bed.

His hands slipped about her to cup her two breasts in his palms as he kissed the shallow hollow where her shoulder and neck met. Her nipples immediately hardened.

"We are lovers now, Maggie mine, and as such we should enjoy each other," Fin said.

His rough thumbs rubbed the two nipples. "I don't want ye fretting over what to do. I want ye to follow yer instincts when we are together like this. There is no wrong or right when lovers are together."

Maggie leaned back against him. Until yesterday no man had ever handled her, but strangely she was not shocked by his actions. Her breasts being cradled in the warmth of his palms felt good. *Very good.* She felt the pressure of his belly against her back.

"Ye will instruct me?" she asked him.

"I will teach ye what pleases me, and ye will tell me honestly what pleases ye, or displeases ye. If we are to pleasure each other, it must be that way. Too many men simply take from their women. I would give as well as take, and have ye do the same."

"Who taught ye such courtesies?" Maggie wanted to know, for she had heard enough from other women to know his behavior was unusual.

"My father, who considered it a privilege to enter my mother's bed. He was many, many years her senior. He might have been her grandsire, but to keep an orphaned lass with no dower safe he wed her, and cherished her. After she died, he would say to me over and over again that a woman who gave herself was a sweeter prize than one roughly taken. In my youth I didn't always listen, but as I grew older, I discovered he was right."

"Then ye have forced women to yer will, my lord?" This was a revelation.

"A man who sells his sword does not always behave as a gentleman, Maggie mine," he told her candidly. "Let us leave it at that, but know I shall never force ye."

"And if I said I wanted ye gone from my bed now, would ye go?" she queried.

"I would, but not until I had tried to convince ye otherwise, love," he replied.

One hand released a breast, and smoothed down her torso to her mons. A finger pressed between her nether lips, finding her love bud. He began to play gently with it.

"Oh!" Maggie squirmed against his hand.

"Do ye like this, sweetheart?" he asked as he pressed a row of kisses over her shoulder. He could feel the sensitive flesh beginning to swell against his finger.

"Aye, Fin, I like it. I like it very much," Maggie admitted. "Please don't stop!"

"I won't for now," he promised, "but there is another way to please this little bud and give ye even more sweetness. Will ye let me show ye?"

"Ummmm, aye, I'd like that," Maggie replied softly, her voice taking on a dreamy quality as she enjoyed their love play.

He slid out from behind her, saying as he did, "Lie back among the pillows, Maggie mine," and when she did, he drew her two legs up and over his broad shoulders.

Maggie gasped, surprised. "Fin!"

"Trust me, love," he told her, and before she might protest, he buried his head between her thighs, his fingers losing themselves among the chestnut curls as he peeled her nether lips open and his tongue found the sensitive swelling bud of her sex. He began to lick at it with gentle, teasing strokes of his tongue.

"Ohh, Fin!" It was as if a fireball had exploded within her. This was surely the wickedest thing that had ever happened to any woman. Coupling was for making bairns. That was what her priestly uncle preached. Why had no one ever said there was such joy in the act? With incredible, wonderful sensations that left every bit of her aflame and ready to burst open, she could indeed feel her juices flowing.

Seeing her ready for even more passion, he covered her body with his own, and guided himself slowly to her entry. With one fluid and smooth motion he pushed into her love sheath. With no barrier to stop him, he filled her completely, and then he began to ride her. Maggie wrapped herself about her husband, half conscious, guided by instinct alone. Every thrust of his cock brought her closer and closer to that elusive something that had escaped her the previous evening on their wedding night. She had no idea what it was she sought, but she moved steadily towards it.

He groaned as he went deeper. She was tight and hot and so very wet. He couldn't seem to get enough of her and almost wept with the pure enjoyment she was giving him so eagerly. He had known some of the finest whores in Edinburgh, France, and England, but he had never known the pleasure that his new wife was giving him.

He found her mouth, and his passionate kisses tried to tell her what he was not ready yet to admit with words.

"Oh, Fin! I die! I die!" Maggie cried as she reached the pinnacle of her delight. She soared into a golden unknown while about her stars exploded. Then with a cry she plunged down into a velvet darkness that rose to softly envelop her.

He felt her sheath tightening and spasming about his cock. He groaned deeply, knowing she was tasting true passion. Then, unable to contain himself, he released his lust into her. *"Maggie mine!"* he cried out as the end weakness overcame him, and then he rolled off her body. But quickly he gathered her into his arms, holding her tightly against his chest as his fiercely beating heart slowly quieted itself.

Maggie came to herself slowly. God's toenail! What had just happened to her? Whatever it was had completely taken over and controlled her. She wasn't certain she liked that, although she had to admit the feelings that had pummeled her had been incredible and wonderful. And she was quickly coming to herself again. She felt his arms about her. What was that thumping? Then she realized it was his heart beating very quickly. Her husband had obviously experienced the same wild emotions as she had. She had not considered a man of experience would react in a similar manner.

"Did ye enjoy this better than last night?" His voice pierced her own thoughts.

"Aye! It was wonderful, and ye did not lie," she responded.

"*Lie to ye?*" He was confused.

"It didn't hurt," Maggie said. "Nay, it hurt not at all. It was as if yer cock and my sheath were made for each other, Fin. We fit together nicely."

"As we are man and wife, they obviously were," he replied dryly, "and we did fit well, Maggie mine, I will agree." Then he laughed.

"What is so funny?" she demanded to know.

"Yer honest tongue," he told her. "I've ne'er had a woman I've lain with speak to me in so candid a manner."

"Perhaps they were more practiced and knowledgeable than I," Maggie said. "Seeing servants fucking lustily in the hay or in the heather does not tell you much other than where the parts should go."

He laughed again. "I suppose not," he agreed. "Well, madam, are you pleased with yer lessons so far?"

"Aye," she told him with a grin. "I hope

there's more to learn, my lord."

"We'll sleep for a bit, and then if yer willing, we will review what ye have learned so far, Maggie mine," he said to her with an answering grin.

"We should pray that the king finds the same happiness with his bride that we are finding with each other," Maggie said softly as she cuddled next to him, her head on his shoulder. "I don't know if we will find that emotion the poets call love, Fingal Stewart, but I know ye like me, and I surely like ye."

"Aye," he agreed with her. "I hope King Jamie finds his happiness too, for his road is a far more difficult one to travel than is ours." He drew the coverlet over them.

In France the month of December seemed to fly by as James Stewart's wedding day approached. He knew what he was doing was madness, but for the first time in his life he actually cared for another human being. His childhood had not been a happy one.

He had lost three brothers and had but two sisters. His flighty English mother had cared more for her own pleasure and position than for her royal son. He had only been seventeen months old when his father had been killed. He had no memory of

James IV at all but what people had told him. Most people had liked his father, and the one trait he had inherited from the previous James was his determination to rule Scotland without any interference from his earls, or from England.

James V had come to France to seek a wife. He would be twenty-five in April, and it was time to marry. He had thought to offer for Marie de Bourbon, the duc de Vendôme's daughter. The girl was more than noble and came with a dower of one hundred thousand gold crowns. Visiting her father's court in disguise, James found the prospective bride small with a hunched back. He departed without revealing himself, leaving his ambassador to explain to the duc that his master was no longer interested.

At the court of King François, however, James Stewart's eye fell upon the king's fifth child, third daughter, Princess Madeleine. Frail from birth, the fifteen-year-old princess had spent most of her life in the mild climate of the Loire region. The French king loved her dearly. When Scotland's king asked for her hand, King François refused.

This child of his heart was too frail to survive the harsh Scottish weather. James Stewart was unhappy to be declined. He wanted a French wife to solidify the auld alliance that had existed for centuries between Scotland and France. He turned his attention in another direction.

Marie de Guise, the duchesse de Longueville, was the daughter of the duc de Guise and his wife, Antoinette de Bourbon-Vendôme. She was three years younger than James Stewart. Marie had recently been widowed, and was the mother of two sons, the second born two months after her husband's death. The Scots king found that he liked her, but she was not ready to be courted or to even consider another marriage.

Late in the autumn, James saw Madeleine de Valois at a court ball again. Drawn back to her, he realized he was in love. And to his surprise, Madeleine admitted her love for him. They went together to King François and pleaded with him for permission to wed. Unable to deny his favorite child her heart's desire, and influenced by his second wife, Eleanor of Austria, the French king finally agreed. The wedding was celebrated on the first day of January at Paris's great cathedral of Notre Dame.

The delicate princess was fortunate in that she did not resemble her father. King François could not under any circumstances be called handsome, his best features being his charm and his power. But his first wife, Queen Claude, had had the same beauty as Madeleine, his favorite daughter. Claude, Duchess of Brittany, had been the daughter of King Louis XII and his wife, Anne of Brittany. Claude was fair to look upon with reddish blond hair and blue eyes. So was Madeleine, but it was her sweetness and firm character that had entangled themselves in James Stewart's cold heart.

For the next few months the young couple were feted and entertained, but their return to Scotland was inevitable. Finally in mid-May the royal couple sailed for Scotland. The young queen had not been well in prior weeks. Exhaustion had been an inescapable result of all the celebrations in their honor. King François knew as he bid his daughter a tender farewell that he should never see her again in this life. He might have regretted his decision to allow her marriage but that she was so very happy, and so very much in love with James Stewart, and he with her.

The voyage was not an easy one, and Queen Madeleine was quite ill by the time their ship reached Leith. Word of the king's arrival spread quickly. The queen could go no farther than Edinburgh. Only the fact that the French king had given his daughter an extremely large dower portion kept the more civilized of the king's lords from complaining aloud of his poor choice of a wife. And plans were already in the works to find a new wife for James Stewart.

When Scotland's king had departed for France the previous summer, he had seen his then-mistress, Janet Munro, married to Matthew Baird, Lord Tweed. James had agreed to acknowledge his child by Janet, and settle a dower portion on it if a female. Lord Tweed had agreed to raise the child as if it were his own. He was not unhappy to have Janet Munro for his wife. Her connection with the king and the generous dower her family provided made her an excellent choice.

And Janet Munro was not unhappy with her new husband. While closer to forty than thirty, he was a satisfactory lover, and told her he expected her to give him bairns eventually. Their home and their income were comfortable. In the very early spring of 1537, Janet gave birth to a daughter who was christened Margaret. Lord Tweed sent word to his king in France of his daughter's birth, but he heard nothing.

"We will travel to Edinburgh when the king returns, for that will be the first place he goes. We will ask for Margaret's portion then," Janet said to her husband. "I want the matter settled before his queen has any bairns."

But when Matthew Baird and his wife, Janet, went to Edinburgh, they found their new queen seriously ill, and the king unable to deal with anything other than his wife. He never left her side, sitting with her for hours on end. Janet Munro was sad for the man who had fathered her child, but she was a practical woman. She wanted what had been promised to her baby daughter. A lass needed a dower to wed respectably.

"I must go to Brae Aisir to my cousin, Fingal Stewart," she told her husband.

"Why?" Lord Tweed asked. "What can he do to help ye resolve this matter?"

"I need to remind the king that it was I who brought Fin to his attention, and thereby gained him another means of support. I want the income James Stewart promised for my Margaret, and only the king can make it so. And if Fin is with me when I ask the king, the matter can be settled immediately."

"What a clever puss ye are, my dear," Lord Tweed said.

"This queen is dying, Matthew," Janet continued. "He is in love with her. Everyone says it. When she dies he will be devastated. Ye don't know him, my lord, but I do. James has never loved anyone in all his life. He is a charming man, but his heart was always a cold one until he met this princess. She is his first, and possibly his only love. He will not be easily amenable to anything after she dies. He will mourn her as deeply as he loves her. He is not a man to do things by halves," Janet said.

"We have not been able to even see him ourselves. Few have," her husband reminded her. "How do ye expect to reach out to him even if yer cousin comes?"

"I'm not certain," Janet admitted, "but I believe I have a way. I have to do this for my wee Margaret's sake. James has not yet received so much as a groat from Fingal. By giving that income to my daughter, it actually costs the king nothing. He will appreciate the subtlety in that, my lord, if I can but point it out to him."

Matthew Baird, Lord Tweed, laughed heartily at his wife's reasoning. "God's nightshirt, Jan, ye are far cleverer than I had realized. Will yer cousin agree?"

"Fingal is a good man," she replied. "He will not refuse me. He will see the wisdom in what I suggest."

"But will the king?" Lord Tweed asked seriously.

CHAPTER 8

It was late spring at Brae Aisir, and the hillsides were green with new growth, and white with new lambs. The frost had finally gone from the ground. The few fields were quickly plowed and planted. Traffic through the Aisir nam Breug had picked up with the better weather. In early June, Fingal Stewart was surprised to be visited by Janet Munro, his cousin, and her husband, Matthew Baird, Lord Tweed. They arrived one bright afternoon, traveling from Edinburgh.

Maggie was delighted to have the company, for there had been no visitors to Brae Aisir in months. And particularly as Lady Tweed was her husband's kinswoman, she welcomed the pair warmly. "Grandsire always enjoys company," she said cheerfully. "And especially that of a pretty woman," Maggie complimented Janet.

"Why, ye are far lovlier than I had anticipated," Janet said frankly. "I suspect if the king had known how fair ye were, he might not have been so generous to our cousin. He's always had an eye for a pretty face." She dismounted her horse.

"Come into the hall," Maggie invited the couple. "Are ye traveling with another purpose, or have ye come to see us especially?" She led them inside the stone house, signaling to her servants to bring wine and biscuits as she invited them to sit.

"I see ye've birthed yer bairn," Fin said as he considered why Janet was here.

"A daughter on March third, baptized Margaret as it is a Stewart family name," Janet said brightly. "She's at Tweed House with her wet nurse. It's safer for so young a bairn. The king has returned. His delicate French queen is dying. I have not seen her; few have. But from what I'm told, she'll not last the summer."

"How tragic!" Maggie exclaimed. "Did ye hear, Grandsire? The young queen is dying, poor lass."

"She was frail to begin with, if one can believe the gossips," the old laird said.

"Aye, it has been said," Janet agreed. She looked to Fingal and to the laird. "My lords, I need yer aid in a certain matter." When he nodded at her, she continued.

"The king promised when he saw me wed

to my good lord that he would provide for our child, for that responsibility is not my husband's. If a lad, the child would be given a living, a priory or monastery as his other sons have received. The king also swore that if the child were a lass, she would be given a small yearly income and a generous dower portion. Alas, with the queen so ill, his promise has not been fulfilled. Now, with her death imminent, I fear the king will be so deep in mourning that he will not want to be troubled by this matter."

"Yer a clever lass, and a good mother to want it settled soon," Dugald Kerr said.

"How can we help ye, Jan?" Fingal Stewart asked.

"Ye promised to give the king a portion of the revenues ye receive from the tolls ye collect from the Aisir nam Breug," Janet Munro said. "But the king could transfer that right to his daughter to meet his obligation. Margaret would be taken care of at no out-of-pocket expense to James."

"Yer cousin is a bold woman to put her hands in our purse, Fin," Maggie said bluntly. She looked straight at Janet Munro when she spoke.

"Ye owe the king in any event," Janet replied stubbornly.

"If he promised yer bairn a living," Maggie snapped, "why not remind him of his promise? While I have heard the king was tightfisted, I was also told he was good to his offspring. Why do ye not solicit him directly and remind him of his promise?"

Janet Munro was surprised that her hostess was so forward, and she wondered why Fingal, her cousin, did not speak up. The look on his face was one of amusement. Did he consider the matter of her child's financial well-being something to be laughed at? But then, to her relief, Lord Stewart did speak up.

"If the king is as deeply in love with his dying wife as has been reported," he began, "he will hardly be in the mood to be reminded of an old obligation to a child born on the wrong side of the blanket. And we do owe him a third of all the tolls we collect to be paid in coin each St. Andrew's Day. That was what was agreed upon when I came to Brae Aisir. Dugald knows it. The king wanted half, only that I bargained him down."

"Why should he have any of our income?" Maggie demanded to know.

"Because he saved Brae Aisir's fate by sending me to be yer husband," Fin told her. "Do ye not think I'm worth a third of the monies we collect each year? I think ye more than worth the two-thirds we retain." He grinned at her.

"Yer a fool, Fingal Stewart," Maggie said. "I'm worth it all!"

"Aye, Maggie mine, ye are," he told her. "Now let us return to Janet's dilemma. I think it an excellent solution that the king's portion from the tolls collected be used to support his daughter. But how can we manage to make such an arrangement? He must be very diverted at the moment with his queen's poor condition."

"He is," Janet said. "Her health is so perilous that she cannot even be moved to Stirling or Linlithgow. She is in the royal apartments in Edinburgh Castle. We can get into the castle. I have a kinsman among the castle guard. And the king's secretary owes me a favor I shall now collect from him. But I need ye with me, Fingal, to assure the king that ye are content with this disposition. Will ye come back to Edinburgh with us?"

"Ye will need *me* as well," Maggie said. "I am the heiress to Brae Aisir."

"But Fingal is yer husband, and surely 'tis his right to make such a decision," Janet Munro said primly. She was a woman of tradition.

Fin laughed aloud. "Nay, Jan, Maggie

must come with us, for she is the heiress, and whatever I now possess I possess through her."

"We must leave on the morrow then," Janet Munro said.

"We will depart the day after," Maggie replied. "Ye are barely past childbed, madam, and have raced into the Borders from the city. Ye and yer horses will have a day of rest before we begin our journey. Now I must go and see to yer comfort while ye are with us, and the cook must be informed there will be two more at the high board this day." With a smile she hurried from the hall.

The laird chuckled. "She has had her way since her birth," he said to their guests. "There is no changing her now."

Fin grinned. "The king gave me quite a responsibility, didn't he? It takes a particular skill to manage it, Cousins."

Dugald Kerr laughed aloud.

"She is very forward," Janet Munro ventured.

"A headstrong lady, I can see," Lord Tweed said with understatement.

"She is known as Mad Maggie," Fin murmured, "and is rather proud of it."

"God's foot!" Janet exclaimed. "And ye put up with it?"

Fingal Stewart smiled knowingly. "She is worth it, Jan. I should have never imagined such a wife as I now have."

"He loves her," the laird murmured softly.

"I have not said it, Dugald," Fin quickly replied.

"But ye do nonetheless," the old man answered, "and I'm glad for it. I shall go to my grave content knowing Maggie is safe with ye."

"Yer an old fraud," Fin said. "Ye won't go to yer grave for years, Dugald Kerr, and we both know it. Ye may fool Maggie, but ye don't fool me."

The laird chuckled, giving his grandson-in-law a broad wink. "Ye'll not tell on me, I hope," he said.

Janet Munro smiled at the repartee between the two men. When she had suggested her cousin to the king's service, she could not have imagined the happiness he would have, but she could see it in his face. She saw it when he teasingly reprimanded his wife and saw it in the warm relationship Fingal Stewart had developed with the laird of Brae Aisir in just under a year. Her cousin had a family now, which was something he had not had in many years. All that was missing were bairns. "Is yer wife with child yet?" she boldly asked Fin.

"Not yet," he said, "but neither of us will disappoint Dugald. She is young yet. Will ye give yer lord bairns, Cousin?"

"Aye," Janet replied. "Margaret is three months old now. In another month or two we shall work harder to give her a brother, for it would please my lord, would it not?"

Matthew Baird nodded. "It would please yer lord very much, Jan," he said.

Fingal Stewart smiled. His cousin had found happiness as well, and he was glad of it. He looked forward to the time they would spend together. The rest of the day and the evening were pleasant. The following day Maggie and Fin took their guests on a ride through a portion of the Aisir nam Breug. Lord Tweed was impressed by the traverse and how it was protected. His wife, however, was enchanted by the multicolored summer flowers that lined the way — yellow and white ox-eyed daisies, common milkwort, Mary's gold, bluebells, and heather.

The following day they departed for Edinburgh, escorted by Iver and a company of a dozen men-at-arms. Fin had sent ahead to Master Boyle, saying that he would expect his house vacated for his arrival and that of his wife and their guests. Two hours before their arrival in the city, and on their second day of travel, Archie and Grizel rode ahead to make certain all was ready. They found Master Boyle eagerly awaiting them.

"I've had the house cleaned, the beds made, and the fires started," he told Archie. "How long do ye think yer master will be here?"

"Two or three days, but no more," Archie answered. "What's yer hurry?"

"I've got two bishops arriving next week, and ye know these churchmen pay well for their lodging. Especially for such a fine house so near the castle."

"We'll be long gone," Archie said. "Lord Stewart wanted to pay his respects to his cousin, the king. We have been told the young queen is failing fast."

"Aye, aye," Master Boyle replied mournfully. " 'Tis a great tragedy. Why he picked such a weak little lass is a mystery."

"She brought a large dower with her for the king, and 'tis rumored he loves her," Archie responded. "Even the mighty fall in love with their wives now and again."

"Then 'tis an even greater tragedy. They say some of the lords are already seeking a suitable second wife for him," Master Boyle confided. "Some are pressing for another Frenchwoman, but others say he would do best with a good Scotswoman. Look how many bairns he's fathered on his own. Six fine sons and two daughters — and all healthy. 'Tis hoped they at least allow the king to mourn before they're putting him to bed with another wife by his side." His curious gaze went to Grizel. "Have ye taken a wife then, Archie? I didn't think ye ever would, but she's a fine-looking woman."

"His wife?" Grizel said, outraged. "As if I would wed with a bandied-legged old fellow! Indeed! I will have ye know that I am my lady's tiring woman, ye nosy little man. Now, if there is nothing more of import ye need to tell us, get ye gone back to from wherever ye have come. Go on with ye! Shoo! Shoo!"

At first surprised, Master Boyle recovered quickly. With a wink at and a sketchy bow to Grizel, he went off chortling, but not before telling Archie, "Now, there's a fine redheaded woman who could well warm a man's bed on a cold night if he were smart enough, and quick enough, to catch her."

Archie laughed aloud.

"Yer neither smart enough nor quick enough," Grizel said darkly. She bustled off to make certain all was truly ready for their master and mistress but not before instructing Archie to go to the cookshop, and the baker. "Is there wine in this house? And see

272

if ye can find some cheese. We must set out some sort of meal, for my lady will be tired and hungry when they arrive."

The travelers arrived in the late afternoon. Janet Munro sent up to the castle to ask if her cousin, the guardsman, would join them later. When he came, they were able to offer him a joint of mutton, bread, cheese, and wine. He ate and drank the meal gratefully, and when he had finished, he looked at Janet, saying, "Ye wish to enter the castle? When?"

"Tomorrow," Janet said. "We will all come to pay our respects to King James at this trying and terrible time for him."

"I will see ye get in," the guardsman told them, "but it's unlikely ye'll get to see the king. He rarely leaves the queen's side. I saw her, ye know, the other day. She was being carried in a litter to the royal chapel of St. Margaret to hear Mass."

"What is she like?" Janet asked eagerly.

"Pretty as a picture," was the reply. "She looks like an angel and is already halfway to heaven, I'm thinking. I hear ye gave Jamie his second daughter."

"Aye," Janet replied casually. "She's a bonnie bairn."

"Come first thing in the morning," the guardsman said. "I'll leave word at the gate for them to expect ye, and yer husband, and . . . ?" He looked at Fin and Maggie.

"The king's cousin, Lord Stewart of Torra, and his wife, Lady Margaret," Janet told her kinsman. "Actually, I believe the king will want to see Lord Stewart."

"It's not up to me," the guardsman replied. "But at least I can get ye into the royal apartments, Janet. And Lord and Lady Stewart," he added, rising from his place and addressing Fin, "I thank ye for yer hospitality, my lord."

Fin nodded. "I thank ye," he replied.

"Will ye carry a message to the king's secretary for me tonight?" Janet asked.

"Of course."

Janet Munro handed the guardsman the letter she had written earlier to the king's secretary. In it she reminded the man of the favor he owed her and requested that he get them an audience with the king within the next two days. The guard went off with Janet Munro's message tucked in his leather jacket. "I can but hope we are successful," Janet said with a small sigh.

In the morning they dressed carefully, Lord Stewart in black velvet canions, black and white striped hose, and a black velvet doublet lined in white satin, its puffed sleeves slashed to show the white. He had never seen any of these garments before, but all Archie would ever say when he asked was that he had come by them honestly. Maggie wore her fine burgundy velvet gown. Her hair, usually worn in a thick plait, was neatly contained in a gold wire caul this day. They rode out with Janet and her husband early. It was a fine June morning.

Edinburgh Castle sat on a craggy hill that jutted out over the town. It had first manifested itself as a wooden fort, built by King Edwin of Northumbria, in the seventh century. He had named it Edwin's Burgh after himself. The Anglo-Saxon princess, Margaret, who had married King Malcolm III, was considered a saint. She had built the chapel. As she lay dying, the castle was being besieged by an army of Highlanders. Her dead body was lowered down the fortress's west wall and taken to Dunfermline Abbey for burial. The great and newest stone building was a banqueting hall that had been built by James IV. The court, however, disliked this castle, for it was extremely cramped. They preferred Holyrood Palace, which was nearby in the city; a confection of witch's cap towers that reminded one of the great châteaus of the Loire Valley but for the background of rugged hills behind it. Holyrood Palace had charm whereas Edinburgh Castle was what it had always been — a great rough fortress.

They crossed the moat, entering into a great open courtyard where their horses were taken. They followed Janet Munro, who knew her way well, walking to the stone building housing the royal quarters. Maggie didn't like it at all. It seemed a cold, hard place for a queen, let alone a dying woman. Inside, it was cramped, and the furnishings spare due to the lack of space.

"Stay here," Janet said as they came into what was obviously an antechamber. "I must find Master MacCulloch." She hurried off, making her way from the antechamber down a narrow corridor and finally stopping at a small door at its end. She knocked, and then without waiting for an answer, stepped into a little chamber. "Good morrow, Allen," she greeted the man at the high writing table.

Allen MacCulloch looked up. He was a colorless man of medium size and girth who would be indistinguishable in a crowd. He considered this to his advantage. "Good morrow, Janet. Yer up quite early," he said, returning her greeting.

"We must see the king, Allen," Janet said. "I know ye've read my message. Ye never leave anything undone." Her eye went to the comfortable chair by the small hearth. "Do ye sleep here?" she wondered aloud.

"When we are here, aye, I do," he said with a brief smile. "Why do ye want to see him, Janet? 'Twill not be easy, for he rarely leaves the queen's side now."

" 'Tis not yer concern why I would see him," Janet Munro said sharply.

"Kinswoman, if ye expect me to work a miracle for ye, and 'twill be a miracle to pry him away for even five minutes, I must know the reason," Master MacCulloch said.

"Remember that I helped ye retain this position when ye were accused of stealing from the privy purse," Janet reminded him. " 'Twas I who watched, and I who learned it was Albert Gunn who was the thief. You would have been hanged instead of Master Gunn had it not been for me, Kinsman."

" 'Tis true, Janet. I owe ye my life, but I still must have some idea of why yer here if I am to gain the king's ear for ye."

Janet Munro sighed. "Very well," she said. "The daughter I bore him in March was promised a dower and income. My husband sent to him telling the king of Margaret's birth, but he has not replied. I know his love for his queen has driven all else from his mind, but the longer we must wait to settle this matter, the less likely it will be settled.

Ye know as well as I do that there are those already seeking a new bride for him. He will mourn, and then be distracted by the search for a new queen. I will never gain what is due my daughter, Allen."

Allen MacCulloch nodded in agreement. "Aye, yer right," he said. "But it hardly seems so urgent a matter that I must disturb the king over it now."

"I have a way to quickly accomplish the deed, Kinsman. I just need to speak with the king for a brief few moments. I understand that not all that was taken from the king's privy purse was returned," Janet murmured softly.

The secretary flushed, then said, "I will get ye yer audience, Janet. But ye must stay here in the castle until I can accomplish it, for when it is possible, ye must go quickly to him, and state yer case. If ye are not available when the king is, there may not be another opportunity. Do ye understand?"

Janet Munro nodded. "I do, Allen, and I thank ye."

"The debt between us will now be paid in full, will it not?" he asked her.

"Aye, it will be," Janet responded. "I am a mother, Kinsman, and I only want what my bairn was promised, nothing more. I'll have little if anything to do with the court after this. My lord wants a few bairns of his own, and I'm yet young enough to give him some sons, and maybe even a daughter or two."

"Where can I find ye?" he asked her.

"In the first antechamber," Janet Munro replied.

"I'll send to ye when it's time," he told her.

"Farewell then, Allen, and thank ye," Janet said as she left the cramped chamber.

"Well?" Lord Stewart said as she rejoined them.

"The secretary says we must remain here until we are called to come. It may be hours until he can find a moment to get us to James, so we must be patient."

"Will I get to see the king?" Maggie asked ingenuously.

Janet Munro was unable to restrain her smile. "Aye, ye will, but remember ye must not speak to him unless he speaks to ye first."

They waited. And they waited. And they waited. The morning passed. The royal quarters were very quiet, for the king had ordered nothing disturb his queen. Now and again a servant would pass through the chamber in which they waited. The long June afternoon faded into a long twilight. Night came. They had not eaten. They had

had nothing to drink but some wine Janet had instructed a serving man to bring them as night finally fell. They spoke little, for there wasn't a great deal to say. Maggie did remark that the hospitality in her grand-father's hall was far better than in the king's.

Finally, two hours past midnight, a page came running into the antechamber. "Are ye Lady Tweed?" he asked of Janet. "Yer to come with me, madam." The page's eyes widened when the two men and the two women got up to follow him. "I was told a lady," he said nervously.

"Ye were not told correctly then," Janet said. "Yer a Leslie, aren't ye, lad? Ye know me, for ye were here when I was last the king's lover. We must all follow ye."

The boy did not argue, for he did indeed know that Janet Munro, now Lady Tweed, had been the king's last mistress before he went off to France to bring back his sickly queen. He led them quickly to a small empty chamber, and then left them.

No one spoke. The door opened suddenly, and James Stewart stepped into the chamber. Maggie followed Janet's lead, curtsying deeply while both men bowed low.

The king raised Janet up by the hand. "A daughter," he said. "Well done, madam. What have ye called her?"

"Margaret, my lord."

James Stewart's glance swung to Fingal Stewart. "Cousin," he greeted him.

Fin bowed again. " 'Tis a bad time, I know, my lord, but I would come to pay my respects to ye and yer queen. I have brought my wife to greet ye as well."

James Stewart's eyes turned to look at Maggie, who curtsied again. "Madam," the king said, "I greet ye."

Looking into the king's stern face, Maggie felt tears begin to slip down her cheeks. "Oh, my good lord," she said to James Stewart, "I am so sorry! 'Tis not fair! 'Tis not!" Then she swallowed, trying to control her tears, and catching up the king's hand, kissed it.

Fingal Stewart struggled to find the words to excuse his wife's outburst, but to everyone's surprise, the king put a comforting arm about Maggie and said, "Nay, madam, it isn't fair, is it? But even a king has no choice but to accept God's will. I thank ye for yer concern. I shall tell my Maddie, for she will be touched." He released his hold on her and said to Fin, "I found ye a good wife, Cousin, when all I meant to do was protect Scotland's interests and well-being."

"Ye did, my lord," Lord Stewart agreed, and drew Maggie to his side.

"My lord," Janet spoke up bravely, "there is one bit of unfinished business between us that should be concluded now. 'Tis why I have invaded yer privacy. 'Tis our daughter's care about which I speak."

"Ah," the king replied, understanding.

"I have a solution, my lord, that with yer permission would solve the matter quickly and fairly: Give the income that is yers and comes from the tolls collected from Aisir nam Breug to Margaret, yer daughter. It really costs ye naught as ye will only receive the first of this tribute in November of this year." Janet looked hopefully at the king. "Ye've never had this income, so ye really lose nothing."

A small smile touched the king's lips. "Yer clever," he said, but then he looked to Fingal Stewart. "Will ye agree to this arrangement, my lord?" he asked him.

"There must be conditions," Fin said slowly, ignoring Janet's gasp of surprise.

"Half of yer portion of the tolls will be used for yer daughter's yearly maintenance. The other half will be deposited with the Kira's bank here in Edinburgh. Those monies reserved will serve as Lady Margaret Stewart's dower portion. The arrangement to cease upon her marriage. Should she die before that time, the coin held by the Kiras will be returned to the royal treasury. The arrangement between the royal Stewarts and the Kerrs of Brae Aisir will be concluded for good and all at that time."

" 'Tis well thought out, my lord," the king said. "Ye have managed to find a way to regain full control of the Aisir nam Breug one day, Fingal. Well done! And 'twill serve my daughter's interest too. She will have a comfortable income and an excellent dower eventually. I will agree to it, as I am certain Lord Tweed and his wife will too." The cold gray eyes turned to look directly at Janet Munro.

"I agree, my lord," Matthew Baird said. "I would be content if all the monies were set aside for Margaret's dower."

" 'Tis generous, my lord," the king remarked, "but I look after my own. Allen MacCullough will see to the arrangement, and I will sign it immediately so ye may all return home knowing the matter is settled. Now I must leave ye, for the queen may be awake again." He dismissed them, but not before taking Maggie by her shoulders and kissing her on both cheeks. "Farewell, madam. I shall always remember your kind heart." Then James Stewart was gone from the chamber.

"Ye might have told me what ye planned,

Cousin," Janet Munro said sharply.

"Yer daughter needs an income and a dower," Fin said. "I helped ye to see that she got it. But the Aisir nam Breug must have one master in Scotland, and not be passed to a second family and then another and another as these lasses wed. The traverse belongs to the Kerr-Stewarts of Brae Aisir and the Netherdale Kerrs. Now we both have what we need, Janet. Be satisfied with what ye have gotten."

"If I had known ye were so damned clever, I would have considered another kinsman for Brae Aisir," Janet said.

Fin laughed. "He wouldn't have been as strong as I am," he boasted. "Nor could he have outrun, outridden, or outfought her."

Janet sniffed, but Maggie was near to laughing. What a wonderfully clever husband her man was. The Kerr-Stewarts of Brae Aisir. She liked the very sound of it, and she knew her grandsire would too. They returned to the antechamber to wait some more. Finally as the early sun began to stain the horizon, Allen MacCullough came into the waiting chamber with two parchments.

"Can any of ye read?" he asked, and when they all nodded he said, "Read the agreement, and then ye will sign them."

The chamber grew silent as the agree-

284

ments were read over. Finally they were ready to sign. A page had come into the room carrying a tray with quills, ink, sealing wax, and the king's seal. Fingal Stewart and Matthew Baird signed the agreements as well as a third copy for the royal records. The king's signature had already been written.

The secretary poured a bit of sealing wax on each parchment, stamping the royal seal into the red mass. When all three parchments had been signed and sealed, he rolled them one by one, tying each roll with a thin black cord.

Allen MacCullough put one of the rolls upon the tray, and the page trotted off.

Then he handed the other two copies to each of the two gentlemen. "This business is now concluded, my lords, my ladies. Ye are free to depart the castle. I have already called for yer horses. They await ye in the courtyard. Good day to ye." He turned and left them.

"A very efficient fellow," Lord Tweed noted. "Why did he owe ye a favor, Jan?"

"I saved his life," she said. "But the debt between us is now paid."

"If we had not been up for a full day and a full night," Maggie remarked, "I'd be ready to leave for the Borders this morning, but I am so tired that all I want is my bed right now. And a good meal."

Her companions agreed. They departed the royal apartments, hurrying to find their horses waiting for them as promised. They made their way from the craggy mount upon which the great castle was situated, and back into the town. At an inn called the Thistle and the Rose they stopped to eat a meal. Seated in a corner of the establishment, Maggie was fascinated to see the different people who came into the inn for food, lodging, and drink. It was her first time in the city, and she was amazed by it all.

They ordered and were served eggs poached in Marsala wine, creamed cod, ham, bacon, oat stir-about with cinnamon, fresh warm bread, cheese, butter, and plum jam. Janet Munro was astounded by the amount of food that Maggie managed to eat. She had never seen a woman eat so much nor one who ate with such relish. She didn't know if she felt admiration or shock at her cousin's young wife.

When they had finished their meal, they departed for Lord Stewart's house where Fingal Stewart told his cousin, and her husband, "Stay as long as you wish, but know that Master Boyle, my agent, has two bishops coming next week on a Tuesday, as I let the house out when I am not here. Maggie and I will leave after we have rested a bit. I don't like leaving Dugald alone for too long. It isn't safe."

"I thank ye for the invitation," Matthew Baird said, "but I know Jan wants to get home to little Margaret. We'll depart on the morrow. I thank ye for yer aid."

"Aye, Fingal, thank ye," Janet Munro said. "Even if yer too clever for me by far."

Lord Stewart laughed. "Fair is fair, Cousin." He kissed her cheek. "Travel safely," he told her. Then he joined Maggie upstairs where she was awaiting him.

His wife flung herself into his arms as he entered their bedchamber. She kissed him heartily. "Thank ye! Thank ye!" she said to him.

"For what?" he asked, his arms going about her.

"For regaining what was ours," she told him. "Ye are surely the cleverest man alive, Fingal Stewart. My grandsire will be very pleased."

"It is only ours again when little Lady Margaret Stewart weds, love," he reminded her. "Until then the king's third is hers, half to her dower, the other half to maintain her."

"But then it is ours again with no interference," Maggie said.

"They have no say in how we manage the Aisir nam Breug, but I will tell you truly that I am glad to have James Stewart's fingers out of our pie," Fin said. "Janet will be content as long as her daughter's share is paid in a timely manner, which I will be certain to do, Maggie mine. Now, let us get to bed, for even I will admit to being tired. If we awaken before dark, then we shall be on our way this very day. I am eager to return home to tell Dugald of what has transpired."

They slept until four in the afternoon, but it was high summer, and the sun would not set before midevening. Archie and Grizel having kept reasonable hours, and having been advised by their master, had them ready to depart. By five o'clock they were riding from the town, and on the road to the Borders. They rode until it was almost dark, and after asking shelter of a cottager, slept in his barn for a few hours until the light came again a little after three in the morning. Maggie wasn't unhappy to eat the hard oatcakes and cheese they carried, for she was as eager as her husband to reach home.

Their journey to Edinburgh had taken

almost three days' riding in a leisurely fashion with several stops each day. But with hard riding, they reached Brae Aisir just as the dark fell the next evening. Going through the village, Maggie felt contentment at the sight of the lights burning in the cottages and some of the clan folk seated outside gossiping in the mild night air. They had sent a man ahead to advise the keep of their arrival, for the drawbridge had already been raised for the night. But as they rode up the hill road, it was slowly lowered, creaking and groaning mightily until it fell into place across the moat. Their horses clomped across the wooden bridge and into the courtyard.

Dugald Kerr was awaiting them. "Welcome home!" he greeted them.

Maggie jumped from her horse's back and ran to him. "Grandsire, wait until ye hear of our adventures! Fin is the cleverest man alive and has done the Kerr-Stewarts a great service. *Kerr-Stewart!* Is not the sound of it grand? That's what Fin called us in the king's presence." She hugged him, kissing his rough cheek. "Tell me that ye like it."

"I do. I do!" the laird told her. "But come into the hall now so ye may tell me everything that transpired. Ye look tired, Maggie."

"I am, but it doesn't matter. I am so glad to be home, Grandsire!"

Learning they had eaten little since their departure from Edinburgh, Busby, the majordomo, saw that plates containing bread with cheese and meat were brought into the hall along with wine. Grizel and Archie had already disappeared, leaving Maggie in the hall with her husband and her grandfather. Dugald Kerr listened as Maggie recited the news of their adventures.

"Ye didn't see the queen?" he asked.

Maggie shook her head. "Only King James, and he looks so sad."

"Yer granddaughter touched the royal heart by weeping and declaring that the queen's condition was not fair," Fin told the laird. "I never knew James could be touched, but he was. I think she may have gained favor with him, which may be to our advantage one day."

"I didn't do it for that!" Maggie declared vehemently.

"I know, but I also know the king's reputation. He doesn't forget a fault or a slight, but he also remembers a kindness. I imagine all about him have been declaring their false sympathy while at the same time slyly seeking his opinion on the sort of new wife he would like. Courtiers say what they know is

290

expected of them in order to gain grace and favor. Maggie, however, just ushered into the king's presence for the first time, wept for a king she didn't know, and a queen she will never know. Her sweetness reached out to him. When we departed the castle, he kissed her on both cheeks," Fin told the laird. Then he turned to his young wife. "Someday ye may need a favor from the king, Maggie mine. I suspect he will remember ye and grant it."

The laird nodded. "Aye, 'tis possible he will."

"I want nothing from the king," Maggie declared.

"Ye may one day, and if not for yerself, for one of yer bairns," Dugald Kerr remarked sagely. "Having yer king's favor is nae a bad thing, lass." He looked to Fin. "Ye did well, my lord. I am now more convinced than ever that ye will be a good master for Brae Aisir, and our clan folk. Regaining our full rights when the king's daughter marries one day was extremely clever. And now that all is settled, I should like ye both to work harder on giving me a great-grandson. I am not young and cannot live forever." He sighed, and then seemed overcome by a bout of severe lassitude.

Fin wanted to laugh, especially as Maggie

flew to her grandfather's side. The laird was a sly old man determined to gain his way in this matter. Fingal Stewart suspected Dugald Kerr was going to live for many a long year. He kept his thoughts to himself, instead saying he thought it was time for them to retire for the night given the lack of sleep they had suffered over the past few days. The laird heartily agreed, and so Fin took his wife to bed in order that they might do their duty by Brae Aisir.

In mid-July, a royal messenger rode to the Borders announcing the death of Queen Madeleine on the seventh day of the month. She had died in the king's arms, the messenger confided, on the night he spent in the hall at Brae Aisir. Madeleine de Valois had been a month shy of her seventeenth birthday. They had buried her at Holyrood Abbey next to the palace of the same name where James Stewart had so desperately wanted to bring his bride. The king was in deepest mourning now, and he would speak with no one other than his confessor. But the hunt had begun for a new queen. The king was twenty-five years old, and while he had no shortage of children — six sons and two daughters — he had no legitimate heirs. A new queen was needed as quickly as she could be found, and once again the hunt turned to France. It was important to maintain the French and Scots alliance against the English. There was only one woman whose birth and breeding made her suitable to be James Stewart's queen. He had considered her previously. It was the beautiful widowed Duchess de Longueville, Marie de Guise, who had birthed two sons for her deceased husband. The Scots diplomatic mission set forth to France.

But Henry Tudor, having divorced one wife, and beheaded a second, had just lost his third queen, Jane Seymour, to a childbed fever. In the market for a fourth bride, he sought to block his nephew from obtaining an important French wife. The English ambassador set forth to press King Henry's suit for Marie de Guise's hand. Still in mourning for her husband, the lady was not pleased by either suit. England's, however, she dismissed immediately.

"I may be a large woman," she was overheard saying, "but I have a little neck."

Similar reactions came from other noble ladies being considered by King Henry.

French king François I did approve of a union between the duchess and James Stewart. He sent to the duc de Guise saying he wanted a match between the Scots king and the duc's widowed daughter. Marie de Guise was distressed by the news. She was not against remarrying, but the thought of leaving her country was not pleasing to her. And there was the matter of her sons, who would have to remain at Longueville as they were their father's heirs.

Neither the duc de Guise nor his widowed daughter could refuse King François's wishes. The duc, however, delayed giving the king the expected answer so his daughter might have time to accept what was inevitable. It was then that James Stewart came out of his mourning. His lovely Madeleine had been dead for six months. He had no choice but to take a new queen, to sire an heir for Scotland. He personally wrote to Marie de Guise in his own hand asking her for her advice concerning his dilemma, saying he hoped very much that she would become his queen. They knew and respected each other, which was as excellent a beginning as any for a good Christian marriage, his missive pointed out.

The correspondence was thoughtful and respectful, even tender. It was James Stewart at his most charming, which he could be when he chose to be. Marie was both pleased and touched by the king of Scotland's letter, for she knew how much he had loved her cousin, Madeleine. His offer was an honorable one, and the fact he had come to her personally rather than leaving it all to the diplomats, King François, and her father, was pleasing to Marie de Guise. It showed a modicum of respect for her, for her position as one of France's premier noblewomen. He made her feel as if the choice was really hers.

She acquiesced gracefully. She knew she would be remarried no matter her own wishes. She remembered James Stewart from their brief encounter the previous year. She realized that she actually liked him. He was quite handsome, educated enough, and from what she had heard and been told, he was a king who knew how to rule. Better his wife and his queen than she be wed at her own king's command to some stranger. Scotland might be a rough, cold land, but she would be its queen, and being a queen was no small matter at all. And she would be helping her own native land by keeping the old alliance between Scotland and France a strong one. May 1538 was the date set.

By the time this news had trickled into the Borders, it was past Twelfth Night. Maggie had found herself pregnant late the previous summer, and she now awaited the birth of her first child, who would be born sometime at the end of March. She did not like being with child. She was not allowed to ride or to practice arms in the keep yard. Her grandfather and her husband treated her like some delicate creature. She found them both extremely annoying. The past few months had not been pleasant ones for the inhabitants of the keep as Maggie constantly made her displeasure with them all known.

"The bairn will be born colicky," Grizel said. "Yer dissatisfaction will distress it."

"At least ye don't predict the creature's sex like Grandsire and Fin," Maggie said irritably. "It's the lad this and the lad that. Did it ever occur to either of them that I might birth a daughter? And I suppose if I do, they will both be waiting to see how quickly Fin can get me with another bairn. I hate this! All of it!"

"It's a wife's duty to give her husband an heir," Grizel said as she had said probably a hundred times before. Her mistress had not had an easy time of it, and she wasn't in the least surprised that a girl used to being so active should object to being cocooned as Maggie was being cocooned. She had been horribly sick during the first months of her confinement. When she had felt better, they had attempted to stop her from walking out of doors for fear she would harm the child in her belly. It was ridiculous, and Grizel had said so very firmly. Then she had been allowed this small form of exercise daily, but it wasn't enough for someone as active as Maggie had always been.

"See to yer duties in the hall," her grand-sire had advised her.

"The household is under control," Maggie replied in a tight voice. "And if ye suggest that I sit at my loom one more time, there will be murder done in the hall this day!" Maggie said, glaring.

"I don't remember yer mam being so difficult or yer grandmother," the laird said.

Her belly was enormous to her eye. The little dent in her navel holding the remnants of the cord that attached her to her own mother in the womb was now thrusting forth. The only comfort she seemed to obtain came strangely from the wretched man who had put her in this untenable position. Fin did not sleep with her now, but he would come to her bedchamber each night, sit upon the bed, and rub her feet and ankles for a good hour. His actions were the only thing that kept Maggie from killing him so he could not put her in this position ever again.

One afternoon when Maggie had actually

managed to walk as far as the village, Midwife Agnes came to her. She had heard of Maggie's dissatisfaction. "There is something ye can ingest after ye give birth to prevent another bairn until yer ready for one," she said in a low and confidential voice.

"Don't let Father David hear ye," Grizel cautioned. "And what do ye know about such things, Agnes Kerr?"

The midwife barked a short laugh. "I'll keep to my business, Sister Grizel, and ye keep to yers," she said.

"I want it!" Maggie said. "Oh dinna fret, Grizel, I'll give Brae Aisir more bairns. But I don't want to have a big belly every year. My lord is both a potent and an enthusiastic lover." Hearing a creaking noise, she turned. "Jesu!" she swore, for someone at the keep had sent a pony cart to return her up the hill. "I can walk, damn it!"

CHAPTER 9

The spring equinox came. The days were longer and brighter. On the last day of March, Maggie gave birth so quickly that there was no time, Grizel later complained, for any proper preparations to be made. Not that they weren't ready for the child. The old carved oak cradle had been brought from the attic to be dusted and polished. A new feather and down mattress had been sewn for it. There were swaddling clothes, and tiny gowns ready for the baby.

Maggie had slept fitfully, for her back ached fiercely. Finally as the sun began to rise, she called to Grizel, who had been sleeping on the trundle. "I need wine," she said, "to ease the pain in my back."

"Yer in labor," Grizel replied. "I'll send for Agnes," and she did.

The midwife came to find Maggie, groaning, her pretty face all squinched up. Quickly she whipped off the coverlet and gave a shriek. "The bairn has gotten itself almost out," she cried. "Push down, my lady, and finish it," Agnes said.

Maggie took a deep breath and then pushed as hard as she could, giving a shriek as she did, for she felt her body relieving itself of its burden. And then to her astonishment she heard the cries of an infant. She had been half sitting against her pillows. Now she leaned forward to see what she might see.

The midwife was lifting the bloodied baby up, her face wreathed in a broad smile. "Ye've done yer duty, Mad Maggie Kerr. 'Tis a lad, and no mistake about it," she said.

The door between her chamber and Fin's was suddenly flung open. Her husband stepped into the room. "I heard a cry," he said. "Is all well here?" He looked about him.

"Yer the father of a fine lad, my lord," Agnes said, holding the squalling infant out for him to see. "Let's get him cleaned up and properly swaddled so he may go down to the hall to greet his clan folk."

Fingal Stewart stared at the wet and red infant in her hands. He was not used to children and thought this one rather noisy with his howling. "Maggie?" he said, turning away from the boy and towards his wife.

"For all her troubles these past months," Grizel told her master, "she birthed the bairn easily. I've never seen a quicker delivery, nor has Agnes. If she hadn't awakened me to fetch her some wine, my lady would have had yer lad without us."

"Maggie mine," he said, seating himself next to her, then taking her hand up and kissing it. "Thank ye for our Jamie," he said.

"*Jamie?* We have not yet discussed his name," Maggie responded.

"Why, lovey, have ye not heard yer grandsire and me in the hall these many months talking about what we would name the lad?" he asked her. "He is James Dugald Kerr, and 'twas decided weeks ago."

"And if this bairn had been a lass?" Maggie wanted to know. She was very angry.

"Why, there was never any doubt this would be a lad," Fingal Stewart told his wife in reasonable tones. "We needed a lad. But had my seed been weakened by ye the night I planted it, I'm certain ye would have had a name to give a female bairn."

Maggie couldn't believe what she was hearing. The words coming out of his mouth could have been her grandfather's. She expected the old man to speak such words. But Fingal Stewart? Her husband, who had been so fair with her until this moment? She was outraged. "Leave me," she said in an icy voice.

The delight of his accomplishment in producing a firstborn son now clouding his judgment, Fin said, "In a moment, Maggie mine. I want to take our Jamie down to the hall. Jesu! The lad has good-size balls on him for one so newborn."

"Get out!" Maggie shouted. "I'll not have ye parading *my son* about a smoky hall boasting to all who will listen. I will only allow Grandsire in this room to see him. Grizel and Agnes will spread the word as to his birth and health. And when I decide, and only then, will David be taken to the hall."

"David? His name is James," Fin said.

"His name is David, after my father, and after my uncle. Add James Dugald to it if ye will, but he is first and foremost David!" Maggie said firmly.

"We'll see what yer grandsire says about that," Fin told her.

"I don't give a damn what Grandsire says," Maggie snapped. "Or ye either for that matter. This is *my* son, *my* firstborn child. Ye did not carry this lad in yer belly for months on end, Fingal Stewart, nor did my grandsire. Yer contribution was to fuck me one fortunate night. And ye enjoyed it as ye always do. The rest of the work was all mine, and I will damned well have a say in naming my son. He will be baptized David James Dugald, and he will be called Davy. Now get out! My son and I need our rest. Yer disturbing us." She waved him away even as Grizel put the swaddled infant into her arms. Maggie looked down at the baby, and was suddenly overwhelmed with a rush of love for her bairn. She had hated the months she had carried him, but seeing him now here cradled against her, she knew she would face a horde of demons to keep him safe.

"Go along, my lord," Grizel told Fin softly. "She'll calm down eventually. Find the laird. Tell him he has a fine new great-grandson, and the Kerr-Stewarts have an heir."

Fin nodded. "The old man will be delighted," he said, and then he left his wife's bedchamber through the same door by which he had come.

"He treated me as if I were some brood-mare," Maggie said darkly. "And how dare Grandsire and he choose my bairn's name? And did ye hear him prattling about how I might have *weakened* his seed and produced a lass?"

The two older women burst out laughing.

"Men can be such fools," Midwife Agnes said. "Especially after the birth of a first son. They behave as if they have done it all themselves."

"I want no more bairns for now, Agnes," Maggie said. "Give me what I will need to prevent conceiving. As long as Davy retains his good health, Fingal Stewart and my grandsire will have to wait until a time of my choosing for another heir."

The midwife nodded. "He must keep from yer bed for several weeks while ye heal and recover. If he is randy, then send him to the miller's daughter. She whores now and again to earn a bit of coin to keep her own bairn, as her da will not help her. She was seduced by a passing peddler several years ago, and the miller has never forgiven her. I give her what I'll be giving ye. I'll bring it in two weeks' time to show ye how to use it."

Maggie nodded. "Is there a woman in the village who can serve as wet nurse to Davy? I'll nurse him myself for a month or two, but then I would give him to another for his nourishment, for I need to get back to my own duties in the yard."

"Yer husband and grandsire will forbid it," Grizel warned.

"I'm not some meek stay-by-the-fire," Maggie replied, "and they should both know that. Having a bairn has not changed me one whit."

Grizel watched with amusement over the next few weeks as Maggie behaved with tender concern over her child. Her grand-sire was so pleased with her that he acqui-esced to her demand that the bairn be named David first.

"Every firstborn son in Scotland is called James for the king," Maggie said. "I would name my son after my father, my uncle, my husband's ancestor. It's fitting for the firstborn of the Kerr-Stewarts to be called David." She cuddled the baby against her.

The laird nodded. "Yer a clever lass," he said.

"I would like the king to be the bairn's godfather," Fingal Stewart ventured. Of late he had become wary of Maggie and her fierce moods.

"I have no objection," Maggie said sweetly.

"I wasn't certain . . ." he began.

"Ye have but to ask me first, my lord," she told him.

A messenger was dispatched to Holyrood, where the king was now in residence, asking if he would consent to be David James Dugald Kerr-Stewart's godfather. The mes-senger returned with an answer in the af-firmative along with the news that James's new queen would be the child's godmother. Of course, little Davy would be baptized immediately for safety's sake with proxies standing in for the king and the queen, who was neither even yet wed to James Stewart nor yet arrived in Scotland.

The old laird nodded, pleased at the king's answer. "He does ye great honor, Fingal," he told Maggie's husband.

" 'Tis not me he honors, Dugald, but yer granddaughter. He recalled Maggie's kindness to him before Queen Madeleine died. He repays us now by giving our son powerful connections for his future."

Maggie smiled to herself at his words. The delight at Davy's birth now easing, her husband seemed to be back to being a thoughtful man. The bairn was six weeks old and thriving when Maggie brought Clara Kerr into the hall as Davy's wet nurse. Both Dugald Kerr and Fingal Stewart were surprised, but Maggie was firm in her intent. As Clara was a respectable woman who had nursed three healthy bairns, but just lost one who was born too early, the laird agreed to the arrangement. If Fingal Stewart was going to disagree, the arrival of a royal messenger put an end to his dissent.

The king would be wed by proxy on the

eighteenth day of May at the great cathedral in Paris where sixteen and a half months ago he had been wed to Madeleine de Valois. Robert, Lord Maxwell, would stand in for the king at this wedding. Then after taking time for her farewells, the bride would be escorted across the sea to her new home where she would be wed again, this time with James Stewart by her side.

It was both a happy and an unhappy time for Marie de Guise. She had lost her younger son, the infant Louis, to a childhood illness just a few months prior. She was forced to leave her elder son, three-year-old François, the boy duc de Longueville, behind in France in their family's care. But ahead of her was a new husband, and hopefully other children, one of whom would be Scotland's next king.

At Brae Aisir, Fingal Stewart was surprised to learn that he and Maggie had been invited to the royal wedding, which would take place at St. Andrews several days after the queen's arrival in Fife. Fingal was not comfortable going, but he knew it was a request he could not refuse. The Kerrs of Brae Aisir were not important, and even his kinship with the king would not have necessarily granted them an invitation to such a stellar event. But go they would.

"Is St. Andrews near Edinburgh?" Maggie asked.

"Not near enough for us to stay in our house," Fin told her.

"Then where are we to stay?" she wanted to know. "We must be someplace with accommodation for Grizel and Archie. Someplace where our clothing can be hung so we do not attend the royal wedding looking like rough, uncouth poor relations."

He couldn't give her an answer because he didn't know himself. Archie, however, as resourceful as ever, had gone to Iver to ask whether any of the men who had come with them originally had connections in St. Andrews. To his surprise, Iver Leslie had the answer to their difficulties.

"My late da's brother owns an inn in St. Andrews," he said. "I'll send to him."

"Ye'll need more than just yer kinship," Archie said. "With the king celebrating his wedding there, there will be money to be made. Ye can't ask yer uncle to forgo his share of the profits. Besides, if ye just send to him, he can easily refuse ye. Ye must go yerself and convince him yer master is important to the king, and must have generous accommodation not just for him, his wife and servants, but for ye and yer men-at-arms as well. I know yer a man of few words, but ye must do this for his lordship."

Iver knew Archie was right. His uncle had always been tight with a groat, and Lord Stewart had the coin to pay for what he wanted. It would not cost his kinsman.

Telling his master that he would ride to St. Andrews and obtain the needed lodging, he departed Brae Aisir. Reaching St. Andrews, he found his uncle's inn near one of the the town's three entries, the South Gate. Iver was relieved to learn his childhood memory had not been imagination. The Anchor and the Cross was large and prosperous looking.

Iver's uncle, Robert Leslie, like his own father, had been born on the wrong side of the blanket in a place called Glenkirk. But he hadn't been neglected as a child. Indeed, he had been taught to read and write and knew his numbers. When he was sixteen, he had left Glenkirk, a small purse hidden in his garments, to find his fortune. He had found it by marrying the daughter of an innkeeper in St. Andrews, working hard for his father-in-law, and was now the master of a most prosperous business.

He greeted his brother's son cautiously. "What do ye want?" he demanded to know of Iver. His tone was suspicious. His brother had outlived two wives so far and delighted in spawning bairns like a randy salmon struggling upstream. Most were lads who had to be provided for, and twice he had sought places for his sons, but Robert Leslie had four lads of his own to see to and could not help his sibling.

The captain laughed. "Peace, Uncle. I am gainfully employed and have come to seek accommodation for my master, his wife, and their retinue for the time of the king's wedding. Lord Stewart can pay handsomely for yer best."

"*Lord Stewart,* ye say. Is he close kin to the king?" the innkeeper asked.

"The king is godfather to my master's new son, and our new queen the godmother," Iver replied, although he did not really answer his uncle's question.

"Indeed, is he now?" Robert Leslie responded. "Well, I suppose I can make room although I was holding several chambers for last-minute arrivals who would have paid handsomely for the beds. Still, a kinsman to the king himself, although God knows half of Scotland has been spawned by the Stewarts' loving nature, is a good guest to serve."

Iver smiled, satisfied, drawing a gold coin from his jacket. "This will hold the accommodation for my master until he arrives," he said, turning the sparkling coin over in his fingers several times. "Now show me the rooms you will give my lord and his lady. Then the coin is yers."

"Follow me," Robert Leslie said. He led his nephew up a flight of stairs, and down to the end of a corridor. Opening the door at the end of the hallway he said, " 'Tis the best I have. A chamber for visitors, one for sleeping, and two small alcoves for the servants. It overlooks my garden, not the street, and is quiet."

Iver stepped into the apartment and looked about. Each chamber had a hearth, which was good, for June could have cold nights here by the sea. But it was clean, and he doubted there was a better accommodation in all of St. Andrews. " 'Twill do," he said, and flipped the coin to his uncle, who caught it. "They'll arrive on the tenth of the month. I'll be with them. Have ye room in yer stables to sleep the men-at-arms?"

"Aye," Robert Leslie said, "but 'twill cost ye more, for the town will be crowded, and any space that can be rented will be."

"Lord Stewart has lived most of his life in Edinburgh," Iver replied. "He knows the way of the world. We are agreed then?"

"We're agreed, Nephew. How is yer da?" he inquired, unable to help himself.

"I wouldn't know," Iver admitted. "I

311

haven't been back to Glenkirk in at least ten years, Uncle. Yer nearer. Do ye never go?"

"When would I have time?" Robert Leslie said. "A man cannot be the landlord of a successful and busy inn and be somewhere else. If ye haven't eaten, come into my kitchens," the innkeeper said, feeling more jovial now that the transaction had been concluded, and the gold coin rested in his pocket. "And make a place for yerself in the stables tonight if ye will."

"I'll take the meal," Iver replied, "but the day isn't half over, and I can be well on my way back to the Borders by nightfall if I leave afterwards."

"Suit yerself, Nephew," Robert Leslie said. "I'll see ye next month then."

Iver was relieved to reach Brae Aisir several days later and report that he had secured a decent lodging for them to stay.

Maggie, usually so sure of herself, was very nervous about going to St. Andrews. Her earlier enthusiasm had suddenly vanished. "Could ye not go without me?" she asked her husband. "Davy is just getting used to Clara's teat, and my milk only just dried up. I haven't got the kind of clothes one would wear to a king's wedding."

"The king has asked us. I am his kin, and

he likes yer kind heart," Fingal said. "This isn't an invitation we can refuse. We will not be among the first rank of guests, Maggie mine. The Gordons of Huntly, the Leslies of Glenkirk, they will be. And while I have avoided the subject for fear of distressing ye, the king has been very hard on several of our border families of late. The Johnsons, the Scotts, the Armstrongs, the Humes, have all suffered his wrath. Anyone he suspects of ties with the Douglases, his hated enemies, is suspect in his eyes. I will not allow the Kerrs to be touched by this behavior. We are asked to the wedding, and we will go. We may not be garbed as well as the earls and their wives, but we shall not bring shame to our name."

Dugald Kerr sat by the hall hearth pretending to doze, but he took in every word Maggie's husband uttered. Fingal Stewart was a blessing to Brae Aisir. He knew that the king, unfamiliar with his kinsman, for Fin had told him so, had had no idea the kind of man he sent into the Borders to wed Maggie Kerr. Nor had he cared. He had only wanted a portion of the revenues from the tolls the Kerrs collected. And he had taken the advice of his current mistress as to whom to send. She, of course, had offered him a member of not only her family, but the king's. It could have been a disaster. And now thanks to his granddaughter's good heart, the Kerrs of Brae Aisir had found favor in the sight of a volatile and fickle monarch. Maggie would go to the wedding if he had to take her himself, the laird decided.

But it was not necessary. When the time came for them to depart for St. Andrews, Maggie's enthusiasm had returned. She bid her grandfather farewell, promising to bring him back a treat of some sort from St. Andrews. "Mayhap a medal blessed in the cathedral to help ease the winter ache in yer bones, Grandsire," she said.

Their trip was relatively uneventful, but as they drew near to the ferry that would take them across the Firth of Forth into Fife, the roads became more crowded with all manner of folk going to St. Andrews. Some were guests, some merchants hoping to sell their wares to the excited folk; others were pickpockets and thieves, and many were going simply to gain a glimpse of the king and the new queen. Summer was almost upon them, and the air hummed with festivity. Iver rode a little ahead of them to secure them places on one of the ferries.

"How many?" the harbor agent demanded to know.

"Lord Stewart, his wife, two servants, fifteen men-at-arms, twenty horses," Iver said. "Official guests for the king's wedding."

The harbor agent nodded. "Yer boat goes out on the hour. Get yer people here." He handed Iver a small slip of parchment. "Don't lose this. Next!"

Iver hurried back to help lead his party to the front of the pushing, chattering crowds. He handed the chit to the seaman seeing to the boarding, and they were waved through, across a gangway, and onto the vessel. Once on board, their men-at-arms saw to the horses, leading them into a sheltered corner on the open deck. The ferry was soon deemed filled, and it was freed from its moorings to slip out into the broad estuary.

Fin was relieved for Maggie's sake that it was a calm sea. There was no strong wind, only enough of a breeze to help them cross the water piloted by the ferry's oarsmen. It was a gray day, however, with a thick canopy of clouds overhead. Lord Stewart knew how both exciting and frightening the trip to St. Andrews was for Maggie. She had never been more than a few miles from her home in all her life. And then suddenly there appeared an impressive fleet of ships making its way towards the same harbor that their ferry was directing itself.

A shout of excitement went up from the captain, and he called down from the small pilothouse where he had been, "My lords! My ladies! 'Tis the king's fleet, and that fine vessel in the middle of it all flying the royal lion pendant is carrying our new queen. Let us have three cheers for our own French Mary!"

And the ferry erupted. "Huzzah! Huzzah! Huzzah!"

And at the same time the ferry full of passengers saluted Marie de Guise, the sun broke through the cloud bank, a golden ray coming forth to seemingly touch the ship upon which she traveled. The ferry passengers gasped, excited, and the talk immediately began to make the rounds of how fortunate an occurrence this obvious show of God's approval was for both King James and for Scotland.

Their ferry reached the other shore before the royal fleet, and the passengers quickly disembarked, for there was still a ride to make to St. Andrews, and if they were not ahead of the queen and her party, they would be delayed for hours. Those in the party from Brae Aisir were swiftly on their way. As they rode to the town Fin told his wife a little about it.

"There has been a town here for as long as anyone can recall," he began. "There are three gates. The North, the South, and the Church. There are two ports. West Port, which opens into South Street, and the Marketgate Port. We're entering through the South Gate. We'll be on South Street, which has many important ecclesiastical buildings."

"Where is our inn?" Maggie wanted to know. "If the queen has set her foot on Scottish soil, then the wedding will be tomorrow or the day after. My gowns need to be hung so the wrinkles are removed. Of course, they will be wed at the cathedral. Is it on South Street too?"

"We'll pass it on the way to the Anchor and the Cross," Fin answered her.

"What an odd name for an inn," Maggie remarked.

"Nay," Fin said. "St. Andrews is the most important church in all of Scotland, and the town is set on the sea."

"Aah," Maggie replied. "I see now. And it is really more dignified than that inn we stayed at last night, the Pig and Pipe," she laughed. "But I loved the sign there with the dancing pig playing on the bagpipe."

"Did ye notice the plaid the pig wore?" her husband said. "It was Hunting Stew-

317

art." And then he laughed too.

They passed through the South Gate, moving down bustling and busy South Street. On the north side of the byway they passed Holy Trinity Church, the oldest in St. Andrews, even older than the great cathedral up ahead. Maggie saw why St. Andrews was thought of as the religious capital of Scotland. They rode past the chapel of the Dominican Friary, the Observantine Franciscan Friary set amid a beautiful garden named Greyfriars after the color of the monks' robes.

The cathedral was the most magnificent church Maggie had ever seen or expected she would ever see. Its dark stone spires soared into the partly cloudy skies above the town. It had great windows of what Fin told her was called stained glass. The glass had come along with the craftsmen to make the cathedral windows from France several hundred years prior when St. Andrews Cathedral had been built. It had taken between the years 1160 and 1318 to complete the structure. When it had been consecrated, King Robert the Bruce had been in attendance.

"Where will the king and queen stay?" Maggie asked, curious.

"They will be in the castle at the north

end of the town on the Firth of Tay," he answered her. "It's not a particularly comfortable dwelling, I'm told, but the bishop has offered it to them, and there is no other place, aside from a priory guesthouse and an inn."

Used to either making what she needed, or purchasing it from a border peddler, Maggie was amazed by the number of shops on South Street. If there was time, she and Grizel would certainly want to at least look in some of them. Several minutes after passing the cathedral they arrived at their inn. Iver had dashed ahead to make certain all was in readiness for Lord Stewart's party. As they dismounted in the inn's courtyard, Robert Leslie came forth to greet them.

The innkeeper bowed low. "I am honored, my lord, to be able to serve the king's own kinsmen," he told Fin.

"I thank ye for making a place for my wife and me," Lord Stewart answered graciously in return. Iver had told him how impressed his uncle had been with the knowledge that his nephew's master was related to James Stewart. And Fin had understood without the captain saying another word that the depth of that relationship had not been probed, yet was accepted as significant by the innkeeper, who needed to know no more than that the king and Iver's master were related.

"Let me show you to your accommodation, my lord," Robert Leslie said as he led them into the inn and up the staircase, then down the hallway to fling open the door to the guest apartment. "We aired it out this morning, my lord, and the fires are ready to start. Shall I send a maid to do it for you?"

"My man can attend to it, thank you, Master Leslie," Fin replied politely.

"There is a tray on the sideboard here in the dayroom with decanters for yer wine and yer whiskey," the innkeeper said. "Is there anything else I can do for ye now?"

"I want a bath," Maggie said in a firm voice.

The innkeeper looked surprised. "A bath, my lady?"

"Ye have a decent tub, I assume," she continued. "Have it set up in my bedchamber by the fire, and filled with hot water. We have been traveling for several days, and I am covered with the dust of the road."

"Very good, my lady," the innkeeper responded. A tub? Did they have a tub? And if they did, where the hell was it? And how much water would have to be heated to fill such a vessel? Providing accommodation for a lady was not going to be as easy as he had